HERE COMES THE SUN

—— A SPLATTER WESTERN ——

JUSTIN M. WOODWARD

DEATH'S HEAD PRESS

Published by Death's Head Press,
an imprint of Dead Sky Publishing, LLC
Miami Beach, Florida
www.deadskypublishing.com

Cover by Luke Spooner

Illustration by Mike Fiorentino, Jr.

Edited by Candace Nola

For Dad, who taught me what a good western is.

Thank you to all of my patient fans who waited for me to come out of my slump after my mom passed. It means the world to me to know you're still behind me. Thank you to Death's Head Press for allowing me to write a volume in their epic splatter western series, and thank you, RJ, for helping me spark an idea.

PROLOGUE

MISS GERALDINE MAYBERRY WOKE with a start as her old cat hissed and batted at the dusty windowpane.

She squinted as she reached for her matches. "Quiet, Rubin." She sighed as she finally found one, striking it against her nightstand and lighting her lantern.

Rubin arched his back, his massive shadow looming on the wall behind him, nearly sending Geraldine into cardiac arrest. "Damn cat," she spat. "What would Fort Whipple be without a noble watchman such as yourself?" The question hung in the air for a moment before Geraldine's smile faded. The cat hadn't seemed to hear her at all.

He looked terrified.

Geraldine stood slowly, the hair on the back of her neck and arms standing on end. Something felt *wrong*. The very air in the room felt too cold, too hostile.

She'd never seen Rubin act this way. Sure, he'd sit in the window and watch people pass by, occasionally chattering away, but never like this—his ears drawn back, the fur on his back standing on end.

There was something else, too.

It has been summer in Fort Whipple for six weeks now, and it got awfully hot in south Texas. But now the windows were fogged over, each breath from Rubin's mouth sending little clouds against the glass.

Geraldine could see her own breath as well. She could feel her heart pounding, could feel her spine aching as her mortal fear seemed to hold her captive. Adrenaline always did that to her—locked her body up, tense.

Why is it so damned cold in here?

She looked to the other side of the bed, to the empty man-shaped indention where Henry had once lay, back before an awful case of pneumonia sent him to an early grave.

What would Henry do right now?

A memory flickered in her mind of a sad, fragile, dying man—delirious from the medication, too much of the sauce, God help him—and the looming reality of his fate.

Don't let anyone take advantage of you, 'dine. You take that gun, take the safety off like I showed you, and—

"You blow the bastard to hell," she whispered, each word a small cloud before her. She shivered and rubbed her arms as she approached the closet. Rubin hissed from the windowsill again.

The closet didn't contain much—just a few shirts Geraldine rarely wore, and her mail-carrier uni-form—which was what she donned at least five days a week, and sometimes as many as seven if her boss, Mr. Walters, was feeling particularly cruel.

In the bottom of the closet were two pairs of shoes, a few of Henry's old things, and an old rifle Henry's father had given them as a wedding gift. She picked up the gun, turned it over in her hands, chambered a round.

You're being foolish, Geraldine. The cat hissing doesn't mean a hill of beans and you know it.

But that thought could never comfort someone like Geraldine Mayberry—someone who could never let *any-thing* be that simple. Call it a survival instinct, call it para-noia.

She didn't have a word for what she felt. The strange sensation was enough to make her go get the gun out of the closet. That was good enough for her.

And the cold...

Something crashed in the kitchen, and Rubin took off in a mad dash of claws and hair. Geraldine let out a little scream and immediately wished she hadn't. With shaking hands, she repositioned the gun in her hands and clicked off the safety as Henry had shown her.

She knew she could do it—shoot someone. It wasn't a question she needed to ask herself anymore. She had no interest in lying to herself; she knew exactly who would come out living if it came down to her and a strange person in *her home.*

With newfound confidence, Geraldine swallowed hard and pointed the rifle in front of her, leading out into the dark hallway. She balanced the lantern on the barrel of the rifle while keeping her aim as steady as she could, despite the uncontrollable shaking in her hands.

The hall was quiet, and every bit as cold as the bedroom, if not colder. A chill ran down Geraldine's spine.

"Wh- who's there?"

She stopped and listened.

Rubin groaned in the kitchen, a noise Geraldine had never heard the old cat make. It was a hostile, hateful sound.

Clutching the rifle tight, she made her way down the hall, wincing as boards creaked under the weight of her feet.

Quiet, Geraldine.

Once she reached the kitchen doorway, she stood with her back to the wall, listening to Rubin hissing and growling from just inside.

Geraldine took in a deep, shaky breath. She could feel the gun trembling slightly in her hands and tightened her grip on the barrel. Once more, she chanced a look around the corner and caught a glimpse of the mirror opposite the coat rack.

There was an old hat perched above a dirty jacket. Geraldine had never seen these clothes before, and immediately she knew.

Someone is *in the house.*

She inspected the mirror further, staring into it from across the kitchen, and began to wonder if her mind was playing tricks on her. She wanted to speak—to threaten whoever it was, and hopefully scare them off—but the words caught in her throat.

The hat... It wasn't hanging from a hook but *floating* in midair. Geraldine raised the gun to the crook of her shoulder, took a ragged breath.

She watched in absolute horror as the clothes moved by themselves. Partly out of fear, and partly from her trembling nerves, Geraldine pulled the trigger and was horrified to hear only a soft click.

Oh God, help me.

In an instant, some dark, terrible thing flew across the kitchen and descended on Geraldine, knocking the gun out of her hands, and sending it clattering to the ground with a loud *clack-clack*. The lantern exploded against the wall behind her in a ball of flame and glass.

"Get off me!" she roared as the thing clawed at her, smashing her face into hot wax and bits of glass. Geraldine screamed a guttural, awful scream as a shard pierced her eye, sending white-hot pain through her entire body. She writhed in pain on the floor as the creature bit down hard on her neck.

It lifted her with inhuman strength, smashing through the ceiling and out into the cool night air. Blood poured down Geraldine's face and into her eyes, making it hard to see the creature that had her in its clutches. She tried to scream but the thing bit down harder on her throat, paralyzing her entirely—save for the sensation of terrible pain, but even that was draining fast. Together they rose, higher and higher, a loud flapping sound reverberated somewhere in the back of Geraldine's consciousness.

This is it.

She knew that now.

Why didn't God help me?

It was the last thought she had before the thing dropped her limp body to the ground, splattering Geraldine Mayberry all over the middle of the street in a pulpy mess.

CHAPTER ONE

SHERIFF THOMAS CREIGHTON SQUINTED against the burning sun as he traveled down a long, dusty road. His old carriage creaked and groaned as it bumped along the rough path.

"Take 'er easy there, Frank," Creighton called to his old horse. He'd had that animal longer than he'd been married to his wife, Mary Ann—and he'd never met a better companion in an animal. Frank chuffed loudly and slowed down a touch.

Creighton reached inside his jacket pocket and pulled out a small flask. He raised the metal to his lips and winced as a torrent of whisky bathed his throat. Drinking on the job wasn't exactly advised, but Creighton didn't see the harm in it every now and then—especially given the current circumstances in town.

Poor Geraldine Mayberry.

What had happened to her was still anyone's guess. It was a perfect example of the exact worst time to be the one everyone in town looks to for answers—when a poor old widow is found plastered all over the middle of the street, her house in shambles.

It wasn't the best way to start a morning.

Creighton shuddered at the mental image of that poor woman's frail corpse, all dry and shriveled like the very life had been sucked out of her. It wasn't right.

It wasn't natural.

Of course, Fort Whipple was in a right panic, and Creighton didn't have any answers. It didn't help that old man Jenkins had called Creighton's office relentlessly all morning.

The damn fool.

Creighton was headed to Jenkins' farm on the outskirts of Fort Whipple. There had been reports of mysterious figures wandering around the pasture for about a week or so.

Creighton knew old man Jenkins was off his rocker, but still, it was his job to investigate these matters, whether he liked it or not.

"Protect and serve, my ass." He spit a wad of chaw outside the carriage. "It's going to be one of those days."

If truth be told, he didn't mind Jenkins all that much, he was a nice enough fella, and he didn't cause any trouble—unless you count calling into the Sheriff's office anytime, day or night, to report some mundane issue or petty crime, of course. The old man's paranoia drove him to fork out the cash for one of maybe three telephones in the whole town.

Creighton recalled the last time he'd come out here. Jenkins had called to complain about teenagers drinking and leaving beer bottles in his pasture. Creighton had told him that unless they catch them in the act, there's not much they can do about it. Of course, Jenkins had replied, *"You can sit out here each night until you catch them. That's what you can do."*

Creighton sighed and rubbed at his temples. Given the tragic fate that had befallen Geraldine Mayberry, he couldn't afford to ignore Jenkins' calls any longer—his superstitious claims might hold weight this time after all.

Fort Whipple had always been—for the most part—a quiet, unassuming place. The worst a typical week had to offer was the occasional fight at the saloon. There had been, of course, a duel or two turned deadly over the years, but that certainly wasn't commonplace.

He reached Jenkins' farm and Creighton pulled gently on the reins. "Whoa, whoa, Frank. Ease it up." The horse did as he was told and brought the cart to a halt. The sheriff reached into a small sack in the seat next to him and retrieved a shiny red apple. Stepping down out of the cart, the sheriff took a bite of the apple and offered the rest to his trusty horse, who neighed in appreciation and took the treat.

"'Bout time you showed up here, Sheriff." Jenkins spit in a large metal pail and barked a dry, humorless laugh. "I take it you been busy."

Creighton tipped his hat toward the old man. "That's right, Ed. Busy. But I'm here now, damnit. What can I do for ya?"

Jenkins stood and waved a hand toward his front door. "Come on in. I got coffee brewing."

The sheriff shuffled toward the old man's house, feeling the alcohol in his legs more than he expected to. This was typical of Jenkins—calling him out here and immediately beginning by wasting his time. "I gotta say, Ed, I appreciate the offer for coffee, but I hope there's more to this than that." He wrinkled his nose as he got closer to the house.

There was an awful stench in the air, and a stiff breeze seemed to bring it right to Creighton's face.

Jenkins held the screen door open for the sheriff. "Oh, there's more. You can bet your ass on that." He turned and spat in the bucket once more before entering the house behind Creighton.

The inside of the house smelled sour, and Creighton figured it was because the place hadn't seen a woman's touch in almost a decade now. The old man's poor wife had died from consumption, and by the state of this place, it wouldn't surprise Creighton if Jenkins was soon to follow her. The whole place stank of dirty dishes, old, rotten food, and bed sheets that likely hadn't been changed since her passing. Creighton couldn't be sure if the reek of booze was coming from the house or from himself.

Jenkins turned to pour some coffee into a couple of mugs. "Take a seat, Sheriff. You're gonna want to be sitting for this."

Creighton pulled out a chair at the table in the center of the room and plopped down. "Jesus, Ed, could you open a window? Smells like something died in here."

Jenkins let out another dry laugh. "Opening the window ain't gonna help one bit, I can assure you of that."

Creighton had no idea what that meant, and chose to ignore it, accepting a coffee from Jenkins, who promptly pulled up a chair across from him.

"How's your wife? And that kid of yours—what was his name? Ambrose?"

Creighton took a sip of the bitter drink and set it down, doing his best not to make a face. "That's right, Ed. And they're both fine. Thanks for asking."

Jenkins nodded emphatically. "Good, good. Glad to hear it." He took a sip from his own mug.

The room seemed to be permeated by an eerie, almost violent silence. It was only in that near-deafening silence that Creighton began to hear something which seemed to come from just outside the back door leading into the pasture. It was a low hum of sorts. Creighton had heard the noise before, but he couldn't quite place it. If for no other reason than to break the tension, he said, "How have you been? Seems awful lonely living all the way out here by yourself."

"It is." Jenkins raised his mug again, his eyes not leaving Creighton's the whole time. "It sure is, Sheriff. Especially when my calls go unanswered and ignored for days on end. Leaves a fella wonderin' if he's all alone in this world." He narrowed his eyes. "Of course, I know that not to be the case, given all the trouble I've had recently."

"Oh, for fuck's sake, Ed. I'm a busy man. I don't have the time to jump through my asshole every time someone cries wolf." Creighton immediately regretted the comment, but he couldn't allow his face to show it.

This is why I shouldn't be drinking on the job.

The old man sat back in his chair and kicked his feet up on his table, revealing blood-soaked boots. "I guess what you're saying is: I need sufficient evidence to back up my claims. Is that what I'm hearing?" Jenkins' face hardened. He looked to Creighton to be a completely different man than he was used to. "Tell me," he continued, "what is it that has you so damned busy in Fort Whipple? One too many drunks at the saloon?"

Creighton took a deep breath. It was far too early to be questioned, especially from this old coot. "If you must know, it appears there's a killer about. Miss Mayberry was found... well, she was found dead in the street early this morning, following reports of loud crashing and screams." He thought for a moment. "*Mutilated*, to be exact. Miss Mayberry had been *mutilated*. Does that answer your fucking question?" He could feel his temper rising, and tried to remember what Mary Ann was always telling him.

When you're angry, count to three. It's what's best for you and me.

Mary Ann was the schoolteacher in town; this wouldn't have been the first, nor the last, time she'd used such silly teaching tools on her own husband. Still, he had to admit; it worked. Creighton counted to three slowly in his head before responding, remembering to inhale as he did so.

Jenkins finished off the rest of his coffee and set his mug on the table with a loud *clank*. He leaned forward so close to Creighton, the sheriff could smell the man's wretched breath, could see the rotten teeth in the back of his mouth. "What if I told you that story doesn't surprise me in the slightest?" His voice was barely audible, a dry, raspy croak.

Again, Creighton could hear a low humming from outside. It seemed to grow louder. He finished his own coffee and set his mug down. "I reckon I'd say, 'put your hands up.'"

Jenkins laughed. It was an ugly, raucous sound. "Come on. I've got something to show you." He stood in one abrupt motion, shoving his chair back a foot or so, and Creighton had—for the briefest of moments—the inclination to reach for his revolver.

Calm down, Tom. You know this man ain't playin' with a full deck.

Then again, he thought, *all the more reason to be cautious.*

Creighton stood and tipped his hat toward the old man. "After you."

"I hope you didn't have a big breakfast," Jenkins said as he opened the back door of the house. "Cause if so, I'm afraid you might just lose it."

The humming wasn't a humming after all; it was a buzzing.

A droning of thousands of tiny wings.

Creighton swatted at one of the little black bastards as it nearly flew into his nose. The stench was almost unbearable now; it was also unmistakable.

Death.

Rotten, putrid, festering death.

A small, undulating black cloud of flies emanated from the barn just behind the house.

"The animals have been going crazy every night this week," Jenkins said, his tone now lacking any of the previous humor and good nature. "I've never known them to act that way. *Never.* Not even when them damn teenagers was comin' out here drinkin' and fuckin.' Always at night, too." They were near the entrance of the barn now, and Creighton had to cover his nose with a handkerchief to keep from getting sick.

"I came out here to milk the cattle three mornings ago and found this." Jenkins nodded toward one of the stalls on the right side of the barn.

Creighton glanced between Jenkins and the stall before slowly stepping toward that side of the barn, still covering his face to avoid the stink and the thick cloud of flies surrounding them. He peered over the railing and was immediately struck with a sense of pure horror.

"She was my best milker," Jenkins said from somewhere far away. He continued on running off at the mouth, but Creighton wasn't listening.

He was transfixed on the putrid thing before him—its skin dried and lifeless, flesh exposed in random places where maggots had worked their way inside. It didn't resemble a cow in the slightest. Creighton noticed something else, too.

There was no blood.

Just like Geraldine Mayberry.

Now Creighton understood why the story of her predicament didn't appear as any real shock to Jenkins. It seemed evident now, someone—or some*thing*—was on the loose in Fort Whipple, and whatever it was, it was malicious.

Violent.

Evil.

Creighton cleared his throat and stepped back. "I think I've seen enough."

"I wish that was the worst of it, Sheriff." Jenkins nodded toward the back of the barn. "When's the last time you got right with the good Lord?"

"Pray at the chapel every Sunday, Ed. You know that. What are you on about?" Creighton wasn't exactly racked with conviction, but he showed up and did his part.

Jenkins spit on the barn floor and swatted a fly away. "What you're about to see ain't natural. If you ask me, it ain't of *this world*." He stepped toward the back of the barn, with Creighton following apprehensively behind.

"After I found my prized heifer in a crumpled heap on the ground the other night, I decided to sit out on the porch the following evening. Just me, a bottle of whisky, and my trusty hunting rifle." They reached the last stall on the left and Jenkins nodded toward the back, where a large goat stood just beyond the shadows, its massive horns curled up and outward. "I was damn near passed out when I saw it—whatever it was that's been killing my livestock. The son of a bitch was creeping around the barn, so I got my rifle and snuck out here."

The goat made a low, rasping sound from its place in the shadows, turning Creighton's blood cold.

Jenkins continued, "I heard that damn goat hollering like he was being skinned alive. I raised my gun, took the best aim I could in the damn dark, and shot the fucker."

"What did it look like?" Creighton asked. "Was it a person, Ed?"

Jenkins shook his head slowly, as if lost in thought. "I can't really say, Sheriff. I saw a shape, I shot, and *poof*, I see a flash of blackness and hear a sound like a wet towel smacking the air. That's it."

The thing stepped out of the shadows just enough for Creighton to get a good look at it, and he immediately wished it hadn't. Much like the cow, the goat's skin was paper-dry and had burst open in places. Its intestines and stomach were exposed and partially dragging the ground as it walked. And the eyes... the eyes were *red*, and they seemed to pierce through the sheriff's very soul. It made a terrible sound, which was somewhere between a bleat and a hissing snake.

Jenkins had been right. This was *unnatural*.

There was something else. As Jenkins looked closer, he saw two marks on the animal's neck, which were identical to the ones he'd seen on Geraldine Mayberry.

What in the hell?

The goat made another hideous sound—its eyes locked on Creighton's, watching his every move. It took a step toward them and into a small ray of sunlight from a nearby window. Immediately, the animal let out a terrible, blood-curdling scream and stepped back into the shadows, shaking and making a low rasping sound.

"Ain't it the worst fuckin' thing you've ever seen in your life?" Jenkins asked as he pulled a six-shooter out from his back pocket. Creighton watched as Jenkins took aim at the goat's head.

"What are you— "

Pow.

The creature groaned and let out another hiss—reminding Creighton of a cat he'd once found stuck in a bear trap as a child. He'd never forgotten the image of his father lifting his rifle and leveling it at that poor animal.

Just as Jenkins did now as he shot again.

And again.

Creighton winced, but he didn't budge—he was fascinated and repulsed at the same time. Boards behind the goat splintered and chunks of dry, spongy brain matter littered the wall and ground, but still, the thing stood. Still, the thing stared at the sheriff—a look of unquenched desire in its eyes. The sheriff watched as flies crawled in and back out of the newly formed bullet holes in the thing's face.

After a few moments, Jenkins turned to Creighton. "Maybe a good, God-fearing man such as yourself can explain to me how *he* could allow such an abomination to walk the earth."

Creighton felt more than a little green as he followed Ed Jenkins out of his barn. He was thankful to be out in the open air again. The old man had been right: Creighton had never seen anything like it in all his years.

Those piercing eyes.

They seemed to be on him even now, burned into his soul.

As if reading Creighton's mind, Jenkins said, "If whatever did that to my animals is the same thing that killed Miss Mayberry, we're in for a world of hurt."

Creighton reached into his shirt pocket and pulled out a hand-rolled cigarette. With a strike of a match, he lit it and inhaled. "I'd have to agree with your assessment, Ed. If I'm honest." He knew there were better things to say. As one of only two people in Fort Whipple even remotely resembling law enforcement, he felt helpless. He wasn't as strong in his faith as some might imagine, but, in that moment, he wanted to get down on his knees and beg for help.

"What the hell do you think it is, Sheriff? Some sort of demon? Native blood-magic, or some of that Louisiana voodoo?"

I need to check on my family. This is serious.

"I hate to say this, Ed, but I've got no earthly idea. At the moment, I'm concerned about the people of Fort Whipple. I'm going to head on into town, see if I can't get a night watch of some sort rounded up. I'd ask if you're interested, but it looks like you've got enough to keep you busy out here." He tipped his hat toward Jenkins. "Stay safe, now."

Jenkins spat. "Yeah, thanks, Tom. I'll do that."

Creighton turned and walked down the drive toward his carriage, where Frank was still waiting patiently.

What is going on around here?

He'd heard stories of natives with strange powers seemingly granted from the very land itself—possibly from whatever gods they worshiped, but he'd never taken any of them seriously. Those were just superstitious stories as far as he was concerned.

Could Jenkins be right?

He turned and waved one last time before Jenkins disappeared back into his house. He snuck a long nip from his flask and shook his head.

Poor bastard.

Out of the corner of his eye, Creighton saw movement from inside his carriage and his hand immediately went to his gun. He snapped the latch on the holster and lifted the revolver. "Don't move!"

Frank neighed, but stayed completely still.

Creighton swayed on his feet. The heat was getting to him, and the booze wasn't helping. "Come out of there with your hands up!"

"It's just me!" The voice was quiet, but firm. Then a small hand appeared from just out of view. Creighton recognized it at once.

Oh, thank God.

"Ambrose! What have I told you about tagging along without permission?" He holstered his weapon quickly and walked over to find his ten-year-old son lying down on the floorboard of his carriage.

Ambrose pulled himself up and hopped out of the carriage. "I'm sorry, Daddy, it's just so boring at home. I want to go on adventures with you. You know that." He mimed shooting a pistol. "Catch all the bad guys." He blew imaginary smoke off the tip of the gun before tipping his hat back with a wink.

"Oh, yeah?" Creighton nodded toward Jenkins' house. "It's not a joke, buddy—what I do. It's dangerous. Do you hear?"

Ambrose looked down at his boots. He shifted a rock around aimlessly under one foot.

"Do you hear?" Creighton repeated, louder this time.

"Yes, sir... but Daddy— "Ambrose reached into the burlap in the back, producing a small .22 he'd received on his eighth birthday. "You don't have anything to worry about."

Ambrose closed one eye and mimed shooting the gun. "I ain't afraid of no boogeyman."

CHAPTER TWO

MAE PHILLIPS FANNED HER face with a menu. The partially crumpled paper had the word *Sally's* printed on the cover. The small eatery was busier than usual, and she should know. She and her friends ate lunch at Sally's nearly daily.

"Did you hear?" Georgia Dawson blurted, hardly trying to keep her voice down, "Sheriff Creighton was headed out to Jenkins' Farm this morning? What do you reckon he's got to do way out there? I mean, a woman has died right here in Fort Whipple!"

A strange quiet fell over the room then, as most of the patrons had overheard Georgia's outburst. The town of Fort Whipple wasn't used to tragedy of this sort—it was typically a fairly quiet place, certainly nobody had ever been found dead in the street, splayed open for all to see like a thanksgiving turkey.

Once the chatter in the place returned to a somewhat normal level, Mae spoke up. "The sheriff has his hands full if Jenkins is being truthful." It wasn't information she was *supposed* to know, but being the jailor's wife had its perks.

She heard things often.

Another of Mae's friends—Lucile Hawthorne—leaned in close. "Oh, do tell." She winked. "We won't repeat it."

At times, Mae wondered if her friends only liked keeping her around because she heard all the gossip from the jailhouse–after all, the conversation tended to head in that direction at one point or another—but deep down, she didn't care too much. It was just nice to have people to talk to—to listen to what she had to say.

"Well," Mae said, leaning in toward Georgia and Lucile and lowering her voice, "Buck says old man Jenkins has called in every day this week." Buck Phillips had been Mae's husband for over thirty years now, and he ran the local jail. He was a hardened, stubborn man, but Mae didn't blame him too much—it was just what she'd come to expect after years of putting up with drunks, violent criminals, and vagrants.

The front door of the eatery swung open as another patron entered and Mae was thankful for the draft of air that rushed in, no matter how small. That was the only thing she didn't like about Sally's—it got terribly hot in the summer. But that was everywhere in Fort Whipple, if Mae was honest. It didn't help that Sally's was so small, however.

"Partner," she heard the new patron say with a tip of his hat.

"Oh my," exclaimed Lucile. "I wonder if it's serious."

Georgia shook her head vehemently. "Whatever it is, it can't be as serious as what happened to poor Geraldine Mayberry." Everyone at the table fell silent for a moment.

"What *did* happen to her, anyway?" Lucile asked. "I mean, does anyone even really know?"

Mae had heard that story as well—it was gruesome and cruel, what had been done to that poor woman. She reached into her handbag and pulled out a pack of cigarettes. It wasn't something women were known for—smoking in public—but Mae Phillips had long since stopped caring what anybody else thought of her.

"Well," she began, a little hesitant, "it was the Wilson's little girl who found her body."

"Oh, my Lord," Georgia exclaimed, "Katy found her? She's not but ten or eleven at most!"

Lucile shook her head in disgust. "That's a shame. That poor little girl..."

"Wait," Georgia said, "wasn't it still dark out when she was found? What was little Katy Wilson doing out and about at that hour?"

Mae plucked a cigarette and lit it. She took a deep drag and let the smoke out through her nose. "It was around three in the morning. Her parents say they heard the commotion too—they live right behind the Mayberry house, you know..." The other two women nodded emphatically, and Mae felt that feeling she'd been searching for. She wasn't proud of it, but she had to admit, she *did* enjoy this—being the one with all the juicy details. It gave her some sort of affirmation she didn't know she needed.

She went on. "But Katy's window is the closest. First, she heard a loud *crash*. That was when she looked out the window." Georgia and Lucile were leaned in so close Mae could nearly feel their breath on her face. "The little girl was *watching* as Geraldine Mayberry's body smashed into the ground like a ton of bricks."

"That's awful," Lucile said.

Mae took another drag from her cigarette. "Some people think she jumped off her roof, but that's impossible. Her body was *destroyed* in the fall. Nobody looks like that after falling fifteen feet. I can tell you that much."

Georgia sipped from her lemon water. "Is it true there was no blood?" She spoke so softly that Mae struggled to hear the question, but it was one she knew would be coming. Both of these women knew Mae's husband was part of the cleanup crew. It was a sort of de facto duty he'd earned somehow—one of the lovely perks of running the jail in such a small town. It wasn't often he was needed for such services, but when the need arose...

"I'm told it was as if she'd been drained by a butcher," Mae said, eliciting small gasps out of her friends. "There's something else, too." She tapped her cigarette into a small silver ashtray, snuffing it out.

She had their undivided attention now.

"Buck says the hole in the ceiling could have only been made from the *inside.*"

The two women's eyes went wide. "That doesn't make any sense," Georgia said. "What could even do something like that?"

Mae shook her head. "I have no earthly idea."

The door swung open again and in walked the local priest, Father Gallagher. He was in his seventies now, and it was starting to show. His skin sagged, giving him the look of an old bulldog. Mae thought that wouldn't have been a bad nickname for the man, either. He was fierce during sermons—a *fire and brimstone* kind of priest.

Father Gallagher was a man who feared God as if he understood what God was truly capable of.

He shuffled by with his head down, but Mae caught a glimpse of his face—sullen, sunken, and a bit sickly. She also couldn't help but notice the way he muttered to himself under his breath.

Lucile nodded toward the old priest. "I bet he has an idea or two about what it could be. But his idea wouldn't exactly be *earthly* either, would it?"

The three of them let out a unanimous, nervous laugh.

The man had a reputation for grandiose, malicious ideas about God and Satan. Anyone who'd attended chapel more than a couple times had surely heard some variation of his 'sleep demon' story—that is, the story of the time Father Gallagher had strayed too far from God—partaking in the drink, fornication, and the like, and had been visited by a small band of demons from Hell in the night.

They grabbed me and pulled me from all directions. Mae remembered the speech perfectly by now. They *stabbed at me with what felt like tiny knives all over my body. And I tried to cry out to Jesus, because I knew that would banish those devils back to HELL...*

"Good morning, Father," Mae could hear Sally, the owner of the business, from somewhere behind the counter. "What will it be today?"

"Coffee. Strong. Thank you."

Georgia leaned in close, her voice barely above a whisper. "He sounds rough."

Mae nodded but looked away from the priest. She couldn't get the demon story out of her head.

... you see, I knew that I had strayed from the GOOD LORD for too long. And he was testing me. Folks, I knew I didn't deserve to live, but that He commanded me to live—and to love him...

"No charge, Father," Mae heard Sally say. She watched her hand over a tall cup of steaming black coffee. "Today has been hard on us all."

The Father bowed slightly, thanked Sally, and quickly walked out the front door, letting it shut loudly behind him.

...and because He doesn't want us to go to Hell and be with SATAN and all of those rotten demons, he has grace when we fall. Those demons were trying to rip out my heart, but I called again, 'JESUS!' Folks, I called to Jesus Christ, our lord and savior, and folks, I want you to know that those demons fell away from me in an instant.

That story had haunted children and adults alike for three decades. Many believed it to be true without question—most, in fact—but of course there were doubters. It was just to the degree they were vocal about it that differed. Mae's own mother had been like that—a skeptic—but she quickly taught her daughter not to question such things openly.

People don't tend to handle questioning of their beliefs very well, especially in the south.

Mae felt a slight tremble creep down her spine and reached for another cigarette.

After leaving Sally's, the three women decided to head to Lucile's house for drinks. None of them particularly wanted to be alone until their husbands came home.

Especially Mae.

Something about seeing Father Gallagher as distressed as he was didn't sit right with her. She'd seen him get worked up, sure, but not like this.

Of course, not like this, someone was brutally murdered right here in town.

It was true. Everyone was rattled. They'd even closed down the schoolhouse for the day. Fort Whipple was a quiet place. Even the natives steered clear of it. Sheriff Creighton had made sure of that.

"Another drink?" Lucile asked. Before Mae could answer, she'd already begun pouring dark liquor into a small glass. "Oops. Too late." She giggled and hiccupped.

Mae gave a nervous chuckle and accepted the drink with a shaky hand. "Thank you."

"Georgia, what about you, hun?"

Georgia fanned herself with her hand. She shook her head slowly. "I don't know. I think I might need to lie down. It's just too hot."

It was true. Even though the sun had been down for more than an hour now, the heat lingered in the house like an unwelcome guest. Of course, the alcohol wasn't helping any, and Mae was already beginning to regret accepting this last drink.

The room was spinning, but her anxiety had all but gone away. She stood and raised her glass high. "To Geraldine Mayberry, may she rest in peace?" She took a gulp of the dark liquid and winced.

A sound at the front door made all three women jump.

"Oh, that's just Hank coming in from work," Lucile said.

Hank Hawthorne ran the local drugstore. Mae knew the store didn't close until six, which meant Buck was likely at home already, worried sick about her.

"Oh, my lord," Mae said, her face flushed, "I've got to get going. It's getting late." She stood and began gathering her things.

Georgia nodded. "Yes, what she said."

The door opened and in stepped Hank. "Evening, ladies."

Mae raised a hand. "Evening. We were just leaving, Georgia and I."

"Ah, don't rush off on account of me," Hank insisted. "Although, if you must go, I could certainly walk you home." He took off his hat and hung it on a small hook behind the door. "It's damn dangerous out there."

"Thank you," Mae said. "But I think we can manage. We'll go together. Right, Georgia?"

"That's right," Georgia said, her voice slurring a little. Mae walked over and offered a hand, helping Georgia off the couch.

Hank nodded. "If you insist."

"They'll be fine," Lucile said. "They live nearly next door to each other, too."

Mae headed for the door, feeling a bit dizzy herself. She'd have to remember to drink some water before bed, or tomorrow would be hell. She turned to thank them for their hospitality. "I'll see you tomorrow, Lucile. Y'all get a good night's sleep."

"See you," Georgia added.

Outside, the streets were empty. A breeze drifted through the buildings, and Mae was thankful for it as they began their walk home. The Hawthorne's didn't live far from Lucile, only a few buildings down. Fort Whipple was relatively small, with most of the residences on one side of town, and the businesses near the far end.

"What d'ya think killed Geraldine, really?" Georgia asked suddenly. It was obvious she'd been meaning to ask it all day.

The drink brings out the honesty in everyone.

Mae stopped walking and faced her friend. She shook her head—partly from exasperation, partly from the drink. "I wish I knew. I don't think anyone does."

"Some people think it's some wild natives, you know." Georgia folded her arms. "Those savage bastards from the wilderness beyond the mountains."

Mae scoffed. She'd heard that theory, of course, but to what extent it held any weight, she honestly didn't know. To her, it seemed like an unfounded assumption. "I don't know, Georgia. Since when can those *savage bastards* fly through ceilings? Did I miss that in my history lessons?"

"Who knows, Mae? They practice some wicked shit up in those foothills. That's what they say. All I'm saying is, I don't trust 'em. Not one bit."

Mae nodded and the two of them continued their walk toward Georgia's house. The poor woman had been a widow for the better part of five years now. Her husband had been crushed in a mining accident and she'd never been the same since. A certain spark she'd once had was long gone, and she had shown no interest in those five years in finding another man.

"Here we are," Mae said, as they reached Georgia's mailbox. "You get in there and lock up now, you hear?"

Georgia nodded slowly, and Mae could see her friend was far more inebriated than herself.

I need to help her to bed, it's the right thing to do.

Mae took a deep breath.

Buck will just have to worry a bit longer.

"Come on, hun, let's get you inside. You're a damn mess."

"Am not," Georgia said with a silly grin. "You are." She walked toward her house and fumbled with her keys, dropping them on the ground and cursing.

"Here, let me help you." Mae knelt down next to Georgia and felt around on the ground for the keys.

"Can't see for shit," Georgia said, her speech slurring even more now.

"I know it." Mae's hands closed around the small metal keys. "Ah, here they are." She stood and helped Georgia to her feet. She tried a key at random and was relieved when the door opened.

"Thank you."

Mae smiled. "Don't you worry about it. I'm glad I can help. Now let's get you to bed."

Before you fall down.

Mae put an arm under her friend's shoulder and helped her walk to her bedroom. She heard sniffling, and realized Georgia was crying. "What's wrong?"

"I'm scared, Mae. I don't want to die like Geraldine, alone and afraid. How do we know I won't fall asleep and never wake up?"

"We don't even know what really happened yet, dear," Mae said. "Maybe it was a freak accident? There has to be a rational explanation for it. But for it to happen again tonight?" Mae shook her head. "Highly unlikely." She didn't believe a word of what she was saying. Truth be told, she was scared herself, but she couldn't let poor Georgia know that.

Georgia nodded slowly. They'd reached the bedroom and Georgia leaned in for a hug. Immediately, Mae could smell the stink of liquor practically radiating off of her. "Thank you for being so kind to me," Georgia said. She brought her face close to Mae's and for a moment, Mae thought she was about to kiss her, but she turned and flopped down on the bed, kicking her shoes off.

"It's no problem," Mae said, backing toward the bedroom doorway. "You get you some sleep, now. We'll talk in the morning."

There was no response, save for the soft snores of a very drunk woman. Mae pitied her, as she stood in the doorway, she couldn't help it.

She's terrified, and she needs someone. Now more than ever.

A wave of guilt suddenly washed over Mae then. She couldn't help but think she could have done better—could have offered her the couch at her and Buck's place, at the very least.

No, you silly woman. That's just the drinks in you, making your judgment sloppy.

She nodded, satisfied with herself.

She'll be just fine.

As quietly as she could, she closed Georgia's bedroom door and made her way back through the house, suddenly very aware of how dark it had become.

The rational side of her knew she didn't have far to go, but still. . .

Images of Geraldine's corpse had painted their way into her mind. Like a pig at the butcher's shop, they'd said.

Drained.

She shivered uncontrollably at the notion and quickly made an effort to think of something—anything—else. She began to sing a tune in her head. It was one she'd heard often as a child, an old church hymn her mother would sing often.

Blood of Jesus
Sweet forgiveness
Blessed savior
He is with us

Mae reached the front door and remembered to lock it before pulling it shut behind her.

Now she was truly alone. If Creighton had a night patrol out—as most of the town had assumed he'd do—they were nowhere to be seen. Suddenly, Mae found herself wishing she'd taken Hank up on his offer to walk her home.

Don't be stupid, you can see your house from here.

She started singing again as she walked. This time out loud, but quietly—if for no other reason than to hear her own voice.

All forgiven
He is risen

Mae stopped dead in her tracks as she felt a gust of wind hit her out of nowhere, accompanied with a loud sound like a sheet smacking in the wind. She looked for the source of the sound but saw nothing.

"H-hello?"

Silence.

Mae was physically unable to move—her spine shot adrenaline down her back and legs, making it feel like she was having a heart attack.

Don't panic. You've been drinking. . . you've—

A loud crash from behind her house seemed to break the hold over her and set her in motion. She took off running toward the back yard, shouting, "Who is that?" All while asking herself what it was she planned to do if she came face-to-face with a would-be attacker.

She rounded the back corner of the house and nearly shouted when she heard a familiar voice—her mother's voice.

Blood. . .of. . . JESUS

Mae stood as still as a jackrabbit staring down the barrel of a gun. She tried to swallow but couldn't seem to figure out how. "M-mother?"

Sweet FORGIVENESS

Mae peered through the darkness. Her house wasn't illuminated in any way. It didn't appear Buck had made it home yet after all. The moon was high in the sky, however, and its light shined just enough for her to see the rocking chair moving to and fro on the porch.

Her heart sank.

The shrill, old voice of her mother continued, nearly shouting now as Mae moved closer.

BLESSED SAVIOR

Mae knew she couldn't be hearing her mother's voice right now. She knew it, but still she moved toward the sound of her voice.

She hadn't heard it in nearly fifteen years.

"Mother, I'm here," Mae said as she approached the rocking chair. She could barely make out a human figure in the chair, but something wasn't right.

A small lantern sat propped near the back door and Mae reached down to pick it up as the *creak-creak* of the rocking chair slowed down. She struck a match and lit the lantern, letting the match fall lifeless to the ground as the lantern illuminated the back porch.

She knew it wasn't her mother's voice.

She knew it.

Still, she moved closer.

And closer still.

Finally, she could see the dark figure more clearly. A man in a long cloak, a cowboy hat atop his head. He had blue eyes and a dark complexion.

He smiled, showing unusually long, sharp teeth on either side of his mouth.

"He is with us," the stranger said in Mae's mother's voice.

It was the last thing she ever heard.

CHAPTER THREE

FREEMAN WATCHED THE TOWN of Fort Whipple from a safe distance, far off in the desert. He'd been camping in nearby caves for the better part of a week on his hunt. It wasn't his first time hunting one of his own kind, but he certainly hoped it would be his last.

When The Order demands it, however...

Freeman had a unique problem of being *too* effective. It was a curse of sorts. Competence was hard to come by—loyalty even more so.

He felt a bitter sadness as he gazed down on that small town of humans, all trying to go about their lives. They had families, children, ambitions, and dreams.

And he's there now. Taking innocent life.

He let out a sigh. It was always a disheartening thing when one of the youths went on a *blood frenzy.* It was an unfortunate rite of passage among their kind.

Some took it well. Others. . . Freeman didn't like to think about them.

About what he'd been made to do.

Not this time.

He'd made up his mind—this time would be different. He'd stop the offender by any means necessary. Of course, he preferred it to be as non-violent as possible.

Although, in Freeman's experience that was rarely the case.

"These people are not ready," he said aloud to no one. He looked down at the dark skin of his arms. It shined almost purple in the glow of the moonlight.

The so-called 'savages' in the hills would be more prepared, but they too would fall to him with ease.

He thought of his home continent of Africa often. It was a beautiful, but dangerous place. Things lurked around every corner in those jungles, ready to tear you apart, limb-by-limb, with no remorse whatsoever. He hadn't lived there long but had visited enough times to know he never wanted to go back.

He reached into a small sack and pulled out a pair of binoculars. He raised them to his eyes and winced at the pain in his left shoulder. The slug had already worked its way out of his skin, but it was still extremely sore. He'd been shot before—several times. Luckily for him, it was never too severe.

Auto-regeneration doesn't work so well if your entire head is blown from your shoulders.

That was speculation on Freeman's part, but he figured it was well-justified speculation at the very least.

The town appeared undisturbed, but Freeman knew it was only a matter of time before *he* struck again. It was inevitable.

The *blood frenzy* was regarded by some as a myth—some bizarre, twisted excuse to go on a killing rampage—but Freeman knew the truth, having gone through it himself at the age of twenty-two. He'd killed fifteen people in New Orleans before he'd been stopped by an elder.

Killed wasn't a strong enough word. Eviscerated was more like it. It was a brutal, terrible thing, which is why Freeman understood the need for it to be stopped. The fifteen lives he'd ended had taken place over a matter of two days. There was no telling how many he'd have killed if he'd been allowed to continue.

If the *blood frenzy* was severe enough, The Order practically *had* to send an elder. They were the only ones strong enough to stop a frenzied adolescent.

Freeman closed his eyes as a light breeze engulfed him. He remembered his teachings as if they had been spoken to him only yesterday. He could see Elder Forsythe in his mind's eye. He had been the first white man—an Englishman, in fact—to treat him as an equal, and Freeman had always been thankful for that.

We have a pact with the humans that goes back centuries.

We do not feed on them, and they do not harm us, nor do they hunt us as in the days of old, nor we them.

It was the old way of doing things—barbaric, bloody, and cruel.

Of course, for The Order to survive—or rather, the individuals in it—if *survive* was even the right word—life still had to be taken. *Blood* still had to be spilled for their nourishment. But Freeman had learned decades earlier that it need not be human blood for survival. It was, however, ideal for peak strength and vitality.

Still, it was against Freeman's moral code, and the code of those he aligned with.

This is why the blood frenzy must be stopped, young Freeman.

He remembered every one of their tenets with ease. They'd been drilled into his head from the day he could first understand what they meant.

Theirs was a peaceful race—and to the extent they *could be*, they were. They only harmed lesser animals, and only when they had to. Freeman felt the pain in his shoulder again, and he pulled off his shirt to inspect the wound. It was a dry, gaping hole.

He didn't heal as fast as he once did. His old bones were frail—his body practically starved of nutrients. Still, he didn't hold any grudge against the old farmer who shot him.

Freeman felt guilty about what he'd done, but he had to feed to survive. Of course, he knew what would make his strength and regenerative abilities return fully, but he refused to break down.

That would make me no better than him.

He shook his head. The adolescent couldn't help himself, Freeman knew that. He could never forget the pure *power* he felt when he was experiencing his own *blood frenzy*.

He'd felt invincible.

But just as he had been stopped by an elder, now he must be the one to put an end to the madness.

Can't keep hiding out here in the wilderness. It's time to act.

A part of him wanted to try to recover more of his health, but it would take too long. He had to act, now.

Before he kills again.

There was something else that worried Freeman, but he was trying not to let it bother him. The kid was getting stronger in his power of suggestion. Freeman could feel it. If he got more adept, he could even turn it against him.

Can't think about that now.

He gathered his things—a knife, a small book, and his binoculars—and shoved them deep into a small rucksack, slinging the strap over his non-injured shoulder.

A horse would have been useful, but deep down he knew it wasn't worth having to control his hunger. Walking would have to do.

There was something else in the back of his mind–namely that he wasn't feeling exactly *young* anymore. He didn't feel as strong as he once had, and it was an unsettling feeling, knowing how formidable he'd been once. How strong the youth was now.

In short, he was not looking forward to what he had to do.

"It has to be done," he said, his voice heavy. "It has to."

As Freeman walked through the desert, he was thankful for the cool night air. His mind drifted to a memory of his own *blood frenzy*. He'd had all the telltale signs of entering the first stages: darkened and raised veins, bloodshot eyes, severe fever, and a general limitation of typical cognitive functions such as reasoning and some motor skills.

Elder Forsythe caught him in his room one day, staring deep into the mirror. Freeman remembered watching in horror as his features morphed in the mirror, some disappearing entirely for several seconds at a time. Forsythe had asked if Freeman was okay, and Freeman had responded, all without a single word spoken aloud.

It was a dead giveaway for an adolescent entering their *frenzy*. The power of suggestion can be understood by mere mortals. Everyone knew that, but to speak back...

It was a sign of maturity.

It was also a sign of impending doom for any poor mortals stuck in the adolescent's wake. The length of the *frenzy* varied from case to case but averaged three to five days—but only because it had been stopped before it could go on longer.

I didn't ask for this.

That had been his mantra during the days leading up to his own *blood frenzy*. He couldn't understand why he should have to endure such a fate.

"I am sorry, young Freeman," Elder Forsythe had said. *"It is rarely chosen voluntarily. But it is our burden."*

"Our burden, indeed."

Freeman moved through the night, smooth and silent, just as he always did. His hope was to catch the rogue on the outskirts of town somewhere, but he could already sense his presence—could already tell he was too late.

He had taken another life, just as Freeman had feared.

He broke into a trot, careful to make sure nobody was around. A familiar sense of dread came over him and he suddenly knew he was standing outside of the right house.

A woman just died, and he's still in there.

It wasn't something Freeman could explain—how he knew it was a woman, or that she was already dead, for that matter. His best guess was it had to do with the transfer of energy from one life force to another.

Being on the hunt always filled Freeman's head with memories of his own killings—it was one of the many reasons he dreaded The Order sending him to complete such tasks. But he owed them his life. They'd taken him in after he'd been turned against his will. They'd taught him how to live a semi-normal life—one veiled in darkness and mystery, nonetheless—and they'd taught him how to survive with an unquenchable bloodthirst.

Upon further investigation, Freeman saw the back door of the house ajar and the rocking chair on the back porch still swaying.

Someone was just out here.

Freeman crossed the yard and crept across the porch. He placed one hand on the back door to steady it as he entered the house—he couldn't chance it squeaking.

The inside of the house was dark, but it wasn't empty. Freeman could sense someone else lurking in the shadows, waiting to strike.

He pressed his back against the wall to his right, standing still as he listened intently.

Where are you?

He waited a moment more, sure he could sense a presence in the house, but he had no idea *where*.

He took a step, wincing as the floorboards creaked beneath his feet.

Whoosh.

Freeman ducked reflexively just as a dark figure with leathery wings shot through the wall right where he'd just been standing, sending broken chunks of wood flying. Freeman wheeled around and drew his knife from his belt, holding it at the ready. "It's time to stop this!" He shouted through the man-shaped hole in the side of the house. "Just come back with me. It doesn't have to be this way."

Freeman stood in silence once more, nervous and apprehensive.

He's stronger than I could ever have imagined.

A loud flapping filled the room, and Freeman dared a glance out, but was pummeled by pure force as his attacker slammed his body into him, sending him flying backwards through the kitchen wall, pinning him to the floor. He felt around for his knife, but quickly realized it had been knocked too far away.

You need to leave, old man. The voice was cruel and harsh.

No, Freeman realized. He hadn't spoken at all—the words had been planted in his mind. It wasn't a trick he saw often, but he'd never heard a voice so clearly through the power of suggestion.

Even in the darkness, Freeman could see the adolescent's features well enough. His face and torso were drenched in blood, his eyes pierced with an intense glow—reminding Freeman of a pale harvest moon.

"I'm trying to save you before it's too late." Freeman shoved the youth off of him and rolled over to where his knife lay, crying out in pain as his attacker slammed a boot down on his wrist.

Don't be foolish. The voice entered Freeman's head with ease. *You are the one in danger here.*

Freeman gathered his strength and twisted his body, grabbing his attacker's ankle and pulling hard, sending him crashing down with a *thud* as his head smacked the hard floor.

In an instant, Freeman had reversed their positions; he now had the youth pinned to the floor, a knife held to his jugular. He had to take this opportunity to try to talk some sense into the kid.

"I'm trying to help you!" Freeman roared. "I've been in your shoes before, and I would have never come out of it if I hadn't been stopped. You don't have to do this, Jace!"

Jace's eyes went wide—first with what looked like fear and dawning realization, but quickly flashing with anger; and without another word, he knocked Freeman off of him in a burst of massive wings and exploded through the roof.

Broken bits of wood rained all over Freeman as he lay there on the kitchen floor, still shaking from the encounter.

This is going to be harder than I anticipated.

But still...there had been something there when he'd used his name. It was a common trick of the elders during a *frenzy*. It can sometimes help them come to their senses—to remember who they are and what they stand for.

Freeman stood slowly, feeling sharp pain in his legs and back. He grimaced, using one hand to support himself on a nearby table.

He got me good.

One thing was certain—he was in no position to chase after Jace right this instant. He needed nourishment. He could smell blood in the air, and knew the woman was nearby.

The search of the house didn't take long. There wasn't much to it—a single bedroom, a small larder, a kitchen, and living area. Half of the house had been destroyed in the confrontation.

Freeman found the woman in the bedroom, and although he'd smelled blood in the air, there was none left in her body at all—so far as he could tell. Her body was a grotesque, shriveled thing sprawled out on bloody sheets. Blood had been sprayed across the walls in a crimson splatter. This was from a severed jugular, Freeman knew. A more experienced killer wouldn't have wasted as much.

Freeman bowed his head out of respect, feeling a tinge of hatred toward his kind.

Men's clothes hung from a hook on the wall, and a pair of work boots sat against the wall. This woman had a husband somewhere, which meant he could be coming home any second now.

He shook his head and sighed. Nobody should have to come home to *this*.

Freeman leaned against the wall, still feeling an intense soreness throughout his body. He needed to feed—that much was apparent now.

Have I gotten too old for this?

That didn't matter now. He took one more look at the corpse on the bed, its jaw broken and twisted, its features distorted and foreign. "I'm sorry." He tipped his hat and walked out of the room.

Freeman limped down the hallway of the poor, dead woman's home, feeling the hunger nearly overtake him. He knew he couldn't afford to go hunt—by the time he'd been able to find a suitable animal, Jace will have killed half the town.

He stepped outside through the hole in the side of the house and stood looking toward town, pondering what The Order would do if they learned of him taking a human life. A part of him wondered if the elders all stayed true to the oath themselves.

He had, and planned to continue to honor it, but it wasn't always easy. Especially now when he needed strength more than ever.

Freeman felt something rub against his leg and looked down at an old-looking, disheveled house cat.

"Well, hello there."

CHAPTER FOUR

AMBROSE CREIGHTON SAT AT the dinner table, staring down at his plate with disinterest. He wasn't feeling exactly *famished* after hearing the horror stories of what had been happening in Fort Whipple. Of course, he'd only heard secondhand accounts, and well-watered-down versions at that. He looked up at his daddy, who still wore his sheriff's uniform. It had been a long day, and he looked exhausted.

"Ambrose, eat your dinner," his mama said in a solemn, almost resigned tone. It was as if she knew she had to try, but that it wouldn't work, anyway.

"Yes, ma'am." He picked up his fork and shoved some peas around, raising it to his mouth and pretending to eat when his parents were only barely looking.

She turned to face Ambrose's daddy. "That goes for you too, Tom. You need to eat something; you look like a stiff breeze could knock you over."

"Probably could." He shook his head slowly. "I'll try, Mary Ann. I'll try. It ain't got nothing to do with your cooking, though, and you know that." He gave a pained smile and picked up a dinner roll.

Ambrose looked down at his own plate and picked at his food.

You're just like your father.

It was something his mama said often. He had begun to wonder if she was onto something. He had always admired his daddy, sure. But how could he not? He had a badge, and people called him 'sir' all the time, and he even had a cool gun he got to tote everywhere. Right now, Ambrose desperately wanted to ask him what he'd seen at that farm earlier that morning—whatever it had been, he hadn't acted quite normal since.

And there had been those gunshots...

"Do you still think it was the right move to close down the schoolhouse for the rest of the week?" his mama asked, likely to break up the silence.

"I don't know, honey," his daddy replied. "After the Wilson girl found. . . well, we just wanted everyone to be with their families. But now I'm not so sure."

"Mmm."

Ambrose could feel the tension in the air—the burning questions his mama wanted to pose but didn't have the gall to ask just yet. After all, if his daddy had wanted to talk about Miss Mayberry or even old man Jenkins and his smelly farm, he would. He knew his mama had these questions because he, too, wanted to ask about them.

But his daddy had never been a man of many words, even in the best of times.

"Daddy," Ambrose said, figuring he'd take his chance, "what do you think attacked Miss Mayberry?"

"I wish I knew, son." He shook his head. "Whatever it was, I'm pretty damn sure it also got to Jenkins' livestock as well." His eyes seemed distant, as if he were remembering something he'd rather not.

Ambrose and his mama exchanged a glance. It seemed they might be able to get more out of his daddy after all.

"What do you mean?" He asked, prodding a little further. "What happened out there?" He knew his daddy would be more likely to give up the details if it was him asking the questions—just as he knew he could sneak along for the trip to Jenkins' Farm without catching too much flack.

His daddy looked out the window, seemingly lost in thought. He didn't say a word for several moments. When he did speak, his voice was hoarse and rough. "I don't want to scare you, buddy, but I've been thinking, and I reckon it's important you understand the severity of what's going on."

"Okay." Ambrose nodded and set his fork down.

"I don't know how much you two have heard about what happened to Miss Mayberry, but it wasn't pretty." He sighed and took a sip of his water. "It was the worst thing I've ever seen in my life—that's as much as I want to say on the state of how she was found."

"I'm sorry you had to deal with that," his mama said. "And I feel for poor Geraldine, too. She was a sweet old lady."

His daddy took a sip from his shirt-pocket flask, wincing. "She was."

Ambrose took a bite of his food. He couldn't explain why, but even hearing his daddy open up a little made him feel better—even if he didn't have all the answers right away.

He'd make everything right.

"Daddy, I heard some boys talking and they said it was the natives taking revenge on the white man for taking their land."

"Who said that?"

Ambrose shrugged. He knew the boys' names but was suddenly very aware that he might have gotten them into trouble. Luckily, his daddy just shook his head and waved a dismissive hand.

"Doesn't matter. People have been sayin' that about every damn thing that happens as long as I can remember. To be honest, I don't think it's them." He rubbed a hand across his face. "I don't even know if it's human."

Ambrose felt the hair on the back of his neck stand up.

His mama let out a strange little noise—like a laugh that turned into a gasp somewhere along the way. "Well. I mean, what do you mean, Tom?" She looked more fearful than Ambrose had seen in a long time. "You mean, some sort of animal is doing all this?"

Her eyes betrayed her fear, Ambrose knew. They pleaded for a simple 'yes.' That was all she wanted from him. But Ambrose knew his daddy well enough to know one thing about him: he didn't lie.

"I don't know."

Ambrose sat on his bed with his legs crossed, staring around his room. He wasn't scared, not particularly. He had his trusty .22 on the bed next to him. He wasn't supposed to take it out of the closet unless daddy or mama said so, but he wasn't taking any chances right now. Not with that *not human* thing running around tearing things to shreds. Ambrose picked up his gun and pointed it toward the window. *"Pew. Pew."*

It wasn't that Ambrose craved danger or violence—it was simply that he had prepared most of his short life for just such an occasion. He'd spent countless days roaming the pastures, shooting groundhogs, squirrels, and rabbits.

You're a damn good shot, boy.

The memory made him smile. His daddy used to joke that it was Ambrose who took *him* shooting. It came natural to him, like a baby deer takes to walking.

His mind flashed to his friend, Katy Wilson. He hadn't had a chance to talk to her about all of this—to check on her and see if she was okay. They'd been friends as long as he could remember.

I wonder what she's doing right now.

Frequently they would lie on the roof of one of their houses and gaze at the stars in the night sky. It was one of his favorite things to do. Having Katy there only made it that much better. They'd talk for hours about any and every subject—it didn't matter what.

Not human.

The phrase entered his mind unexpectedly and forcibly every few minutes. It definitely bothered him—mostly because he didn't want to imagine the animal capable of doing *that.*

Without giving it another thought, Ambrose placed his feet on the floor, grabbed his .22 off his bed, and moved to the window, shoving the gun into his back pocket. Maybe going outside right now wasn't the best idea he'd ever had, but he felt he'd go crazy cooped up in his room with his troubled friend on his mind.

He made an effort to be as quiet as possible as he worked the window open. But despite his efforts, the window creaked anyway. The house was an old one, and the wood had seen better days. He stood still in the near-darkness, listening for any sign that someone had heard him trying to sneak out.

All clear.

He wasn't even sure whether his parents were asleep or not. His daddy had looked pretty tired at dinner. Still, if he knew him at all he figured he'd be somewhere near the front door, sitting up in a chair with a gun across his lap. That was his job, both at day and at night—he protected people.

Ambrose slipped a leg out of the window as he had done what felt like a million times. His foot caught on a familiar ledge, and he worked his other foot out, holding on to the window frame for support. Once both of his feet were firmly planted on the ledge below, Ambrose pulled himself up and onto the roof with one swift yank. He reached back to make sure the gun hadn't fallen out of his pocket and grabbed it to hold at the ready.

He gave the street below and the buildings around a cursory glance. Everything seemed normal—eerily quiet, in fact.

The Wilson house wasn't far, only three houses away. If Ambrose was discreet enough—as he usually was—he could sneak over to her window in a matter of minutes without waking or disturbing anyone.

He moved along the tops of the houses, his movement smooth and deliberate. He made sure to avoid stepping above his parent's bedroom, and—just to be safe—the living room as well. As he moved along the rooftops, he glanced repeatedly to the street to make sure he wasn't being followed by anyone.

Or any*thing.*

Ambrose shuddered and willed himself to think of something else.

The Wilsons' house was dark, but Ambrose figured Katy would still be awake. This was right around the time they usually met up. He slinked quietly across the top of her bedroom, hanging down by his waist to tap on the glass below.

Tap, ta-tap tap. It was their signature knock.

"Hey, Katy, it's me," he whispered.

Almost immediately, a small light flicked on from inside the bedroom. Ambrose could hear the soft shuffling of Katy's feet as she walked over to the window.

Whoosh.

Katy poked her head out and looked up. "Of course, it's you, dummy. Who else knows the secret knock?"

"Shut up."

"You shut up." Katy smiled. "Come on, get in here before something eats you."

Ambrose shuffled down off the roof and swung into Katy's room as quietly as possible. "Not funny."

"You're not the one who had to see... that." Katy's eyes fell to the floor.

Ambrose hugged her. "I'm sorry. I wanted to come see you. I figured you'd wanna talk about it."

Katy sat on the end of her bed and crossed her arms. "It was awful. It was— "she seemed to genuinely struggle for the right word. "It was the worst thing I've ever seen in my life." She finally said in a quiet tone.

Ambrose nodded. He didn't know what to say. There were, of course, plenty of questions he wanted to ask her—little details he was dying to know, but even at his young age, he had enough sense to know now wasn't the time for that.

Luckily for him, she was in the telling mood. "Some people say she jumped off her roof," she said, her voice shaking a little. "But I know that's not true." She stood and walked over to the window. "Come on, let's get some fresh air. I'd rather not have to whisper all this."

Ambrose followed Katy to the roof the same way they'd done for years. She was right, the fresh air felt great, and it would be nice to be able to talk without her parents catching him in her room.

The two of them sat down on the side of the roof overlooking the town. There was Sally's, one of his mama's favorite places, the barbershop, and the jailhouse a few buildings down from that. Fort Whipple wasn't big by any means, but it was growing more and more each year. Ambrose heard that kind of talk at the dinner table often.

May have to work for me as my number one deputy one day, champ.

Ambrose smiled at the memory, but the smile quickly faded as Katy continued her story.

"Anyway, I was lying in bed when I heard shouting coming from the Mayberry house. It was awful, more screeching than shouting. I hopped out of bed and went to the window. I couldn't see anything at first, but I heard a loud *crashing* sound unlike anything I'd ever heard before." She mimicked breaking a stick in her hands. "It was like a tree snapped in half like it was nothing, and when I say it was loud, I mean it almost gave me a heart attack, Amby."

Ambrose blushed. He didn't mind the nickname, but only when Katy used it—and especially only if they were alone. He certainly didn't want his friends catching wind of it.

"Then what happened?"

Katy brushed a strand of hair behind her ear and shifted to face Ambrose. "Well, I opened my window. I guess I thought I'd get a better view or something." She made a sour face. "Turns out I wasn't wrong. And this goes back to what I was saying before. I saw that woman *fall*. It wasn't like she jumped from the roof. She was never *on the roof.* Whatever it was that killed her, it dropped her from somewhere up there." She pointed up at the sky.

Ambrose felt a jolt of nervous energy run down his spine. He suddenly found himself wishing he hadn't snuck out of the house. "M-my daddy— "he shook his head. "My dad says he has good reason to believe the livestock on Jenkins' Farm have been getting killed by the same thing."

"Something is turning cattle into raisins too?"

Ambrose frowned. "Raisins?"

"He didn't tell you what the bodies looked like? What Miss Mayberry looked like?"

Ambrose shook his head. "Well, not really, no."

Katy reached over and patted him on the knee. "That's probably for the best."

"Ah, come on, tell me."

"Are you sure? Because I haven't slept a wink since. I probably won't sleep for at least the next four years, and that's if I'm lucky."

Ambrose let out a little laugh. "Yeah, I'm sure." He pulled his gun out of his back pocket and set it on the roof next to him. "I need to know what I'm up against."

Katy thought for a moment. "It didn't look like a normal dead person—like at the funeral home, you know, in the casket. Those people look like normal people, only sleeping. For the most part, anyway. But not miss Mayberry. She looked like a lifeless rag doll person." Katy sighed. "It was... she looked like one of those mummies from our history books. Her face was like a gross skeleton with the skin pulled tight." She shook her head. "I'll never forget that image, like she was screaming long after she died."

Ambrose didn't understand. Had Katy actually seen these things? Was it possible she dreamed some of it? It didn't make any sense. How could Miss Mayberry turn into a mummy, or fly through the air?

"It's fine. I don't expect you to believe me," Katy said, as if she'd read his mind.

"It's not that," Ambrose said, "I just don't know what to make of it is all."

"You're telling me."

The two of them sat in silence for a long time. Ambrose gazed at the stars, imagining what sort of thing could do what had been done to Miss Mayberry.

"Thank you for coming to check on me," Katy said, finally.

"Of course. I'm glad you're okay, even though you won't sleep for the next several years."

Katy laughed. "Speaking of that, I probably need to head inside. After last night, they're likely to poke their heads in and check on me a couple times."

"Yeah, okay. I probably need to get home, too." Ambrose followed Katy back to her window and wished her a goodnight.

As he made his way back home, he felt a lot better about things. Seeing Katy usually did that for him. Most of his friends gave him grief about it, calling her his girlfriend. He didn't know if that's what she was or not, but ultimately, he didn't care, either.

The warm feeling at his core faded in an instant when he saw the shadowy figure of a tall, dark man slip behind a building, just out of the corner of his eye. Ambrose reached back and grabbed his .22 pistol. He trained the gun on the spot where the man had disappeared out of sight.

A nagging feeling in the pit of his stomach pulled at him. He'd begun to wonder if he'd imagined the whole thing.

No, he suddenly *knew* he'd imagined it, he decided.

You didn't see anything.

It was almost as if a voice had spoken it from somewhere inside his mind, reassuring him everything was fine. He put the pistol back in his pocket and continued on his rooftop journey back home, feeling a bit strange, almost as if he were being watched.

No, that was all in my head.

But was it? How was he so sure?

Because you know. It was just a shadow. You weren't looking directly at it, anyway.

"Get out of my head!" Ambrose shouted. He reached for his .22 and shouted in pain as something slammed hard into his arm, knocking the gun out of his grip and sending it toppling across the rooftop.

Ambrose shouted in pain as he fell and began rolling side over side, finally stopping when his hands gripped the gutters over the edge of his house. His feet dangled and slapped against his parent's bedroom window with a loud *thud.*

Even in the darkness, Ambrose could see the thing's massive wings protruding from its back as it took a step toward him. He could hear its awful breathing. It seemed to be laughing at him.

Ambrose could see his pistol now—just an arm's reach away. His fingers shook from holding on, but he knew he'd break his legs if he fell from this height.

Don't even think about it.

There was that voice again. Ambrose had no doubts about where it was coming from. It wasn't spoken to him but *transmitted into his consciousness.*

The creature lunged toward the gun, and Ambrose took his chance, doing the same. He swung his leg over the side of the roof with all his might, diving toward the pistol with his entire bodyweight. His hand slipped around the metallic grip just before a colossal force collided with his side, knocking him off the roof. Together, they fell into a tangled mess, hitting the ground hard with a loud *smack.*

Ambrose lay still in shocked disbelief. How had he not been hurt in the fall?

He didn't have to wonder long, as he could feel the thing beneath him wrap its terrible hands around his throat. It pushed his head to the side and came in close, like it wanted to whisper in his ear.

No, it wants to bite me.

He couldn't explain how he knew this, but he did, in the same way he knew the voice heard its voice in his head was coming from the creature.

Ambrose reached behind him, placed the barrel of his pistol in his attacker's face, and pulled the trigger.

A scream unlike anything he'd ever heard before erupted in his ear as the thing shoved Ambrose off in an explosion of erupting wings. Ambrose scrambled to his feet, took aim, and shot three more times before the thing disappeared out of view.

Ambrose turned and saw his daddy standing there—still in uniform—holding a shotgun, his eyes as big as saucers. Ambrose tried to speak, but he still hadn't caught his breath. He could only wheeze and point.

"I saw it." His daddy shook his head. "I saw the goddamn son of a bitching thing."

Ambrose nodded. He'd never heard his daddy so worked up.

"I shot it in the face, Daddy."

"I know you did, Son."

"It kept moving, Daddy."

"I know it."

The two of them stood in silence a moment longer before the quiet was broken with a bloodcurdling scream of agony.

"Creighton!" There was no doubt who it was—Ambrose had known Buck Phillips his entire life. He and his wife were good friends of his parents.'

"Creighton, *it got Mae!*"

Ambrose felt his body stiffen, and he could see the visible hurt on his daddy's face.

Buck Phillips came stumbling toward them, carrying a gun at the ready. "My house is destroyed, and Mae is dead!" he shouted, tears flowing down his face. "She's *dead,* Sheriff!"

His daddy nodded. "I'll put together a search party, Buck, and we'll get this motherfucker if it's the last thing we do."

CHAPTER FIVE

FATHER GALLAGHER FLIPPED FURIOUSLY through book after book in futility. He'd spent an afternoon pouring over massive tomes from his personal library provided by the church. That was where he was now—in the chapel, surrounded by lit candles of various sizes, holy water, and an array of wooden crosses he'd sharpened into fine points on the long end.

He'd been warning of this day for a long time, but no one ever listened.

No one heeded his message—if they had, they wouldn't have found themselves in such a predicament. He bowed his head for what seemed like the thousandth time that day.

"Father, please forgive them, for they know not what they do..."

He made the sign of the Trinity over his chest and looked up at the much larger cross before him. It was an impressive structure Father Gallagher had made with his own hands—with the help of some skilled metalworkers who attended weekly chapel. He was proud of it, of what it represented.

It was no mystery—what was happening in Fort Whipple. He'd foreseen this town's fiery demise long ago, but still, he had to *try* to steer the ship in the right direction.

He had to.

But it was too late for this old town now.

Fort Whipple needed to be cleansed, and much like the world preceding the great flood, there was nothing salvageable here.

Only Father Gallagher knew the cleansing would come in a different form. There would be no great flood—no, that would have been too easy.

He shook his head and sighed. No, Fort Whipple had chosen the slow, pestilence-ridden, rotting death of self-deception, and God would have no say in the matter. He would merely turn his back on them during their time of need—much like the people had done to him.

Father Gallagher understood this, yet he still obeyed. He stayed despite the knowledge of his impending doom; he had long ago put aside any notion of self-preservation, along with the anxieties and worries of day-to-day life.

It was all useless. *His* will would be done one way or the other. There was no sense in running from it—that would mean abandoning everyone who depended on him.

No, he wasn't running; but that didn't mean he couldn't attempt to defend himself. His hand drifted to the small metal cross which hung from his neck. He closed his eyes.

"Our father, who art in heaven..."

He shook his head. "Nonsense," he whispered under his breath.

God wasn't listening anymore.

Maybe it was a force of habit, but he couldn't imagine giving up the prayer altogether.

But maybe you should...

Father Gallagher twitched in his seat. He had of course *heard* the voice in his head—the evil, silky voice of one of Satan's minions. He was not surprised to be tested during such a hardship. He'd expected it.

He stood and spoke with authority to the empty chapel. "You shall not have me, foul demon!" He gazed around the room as his voice reverberated all the way up the bell tower above—the tower he rarely visited anymore, it seemed to call to him now.

It begged him to come and visit.

Father Gallagher mumbled to himself as he sat back down with uneasy resignation. His eyes searched the room for a sign of anything out of place. Candlelight flickered and danced on the walls, casting long, dark shadows across the chapel. He tried to ignore the undulating shadows as best he could, but still, they taunted him.

It was merely a sign that he was getting closer to God. The devil himself felt threatened by Father Gallagher—that was it. It explained everything.

If you're so close to God, why do you feel so compelled to end it all?

"Stop it!" He shouted, tears filling his eyes. "Get out of my head, damn you!"

Is it because you'd like to meet him face-to-face tonight?

In a fit of rage, the old priest slammed the book shut, a fire alight behind his eyes. "In the good and holy name of Jesus Christ, I command you to reveal yourself, demon!"

Father Gallagher's eyes darted around the chapel as he waited for a response—for some dark, wicked thing to appear in front of him and grab him by the throat. Or possibly he would feel the cold, stale breath on the back of his neck just before a clawed-hand caught him on the cheek, ripping his face open.

Being a man in his position, he had to be prepared to face these attacks.

He had to be willing to die.

It wasn't something he wanted—to die a painful, terrifying death in the house of God—but if it were *required*, well. . .

He glanced up to the cross again. The Christ had suffered for all of humanity, why should he be any different? How could the old priest think he was any less deserving of such a fate?

A loud creak startled Father Gallagher nearly out of his skin as the chapel doors suddenly burst open. He ducked as a massive gust of wind blew through the building and papers began to fly around the room; each candle around him began to die out in rapid succession.

"Back to Hell, damn you!" The priest grabbed the cross around his neck and ripped it off, sending pieces of the golden chain clinking to the floor. Holding it high, he turned around in a slow circle as pages continued to fly around him. More and more candles went out until there was barely enough light to make out a lone, shadowy figure approaching him.

Father Gallagher's voice shook as he recited the prayer he'd memorized so many years ago. "Yea, though I walk through the valley of the shadow of death..."

He let out another startled cry as a large book fell off his study and landed open on the floor, its pages flipping—*no, not flipping, flapping in the wind.*

Just the wind...

A voice whispered in his head. A small tickle at first, but quickly growing—*it's not just the wind, and you know it, old man.*

He stared at the book on the floor, suddenly realizing the wind had stopped completely. He wheeled around and could no longer see any obscure figure, no shadows.

There was only the book now. It called to him.

It had knowledge to share.

Father Gallagher trembled. Everything in him knew he should leave now—he could turn his back on this town and move on with his life. Of course, that was entirely fantasy.

He knew he could no more stop himself from investigating the book than a tumbleweed could stop itself from blowing in the wind.

Slowly, he approached the open tome, each step a tedious endeavor—like wading through a dark, dense swamp. The eerie silence of the room seemed to mock him.

The room had grown incredibly dark, the Father could only find a single candle that hadn't yet gone out. He grabbed it with an outstretched, unsteady hand and held it out in front of him. Its glow wasn't much, but it was better than nothing.

On shaky legs, the father knelt low to the floor, squinting down at the pages. He saw a drawing of a cloaked figure but couldn't make out the inscription.

The room had gone quiet, and the silence hung thick in the air. Each labored, nervous breath could be heard aloud—along with the loud thumping of the old man's heart.

Father Gallagher lifted the book with one hand and held the candle close with the other.

The word at the top of the page caused him to drop the book, sending it to the floor with a loud *WHAP*. He screamed as the candlelight went out suddenly. Backing into a corner, he shielded his neck with both hands as he tried to decide where to go, what to do.

Then his decision was made for him. He looked to the doors and saw the thing standing there; cloaked, eyes piercing.

Watching its prey.

Father Gallagher didn't have to wonder what the creature was anymore. His research had led him in the right direction, only now he knew his death was imminent.

I won't make it easy for it.

He bowed his head slightly, whispering a quiet prayer, never taking his eyes off the thing. A chill ran down the old man's spine as he watched a massive pair of leathery wings slowly unfold from the creature's back.

"My God..." It came out of his mouth in a quiet whisper.

Suddenly, the voice returned inside his mind. It spoke a single sentence in a seductive voice, seeming to pull at him. *God hasn't responded once in your life.*

Father Gallagher was terrified. He stumbled over to the table and grabbed a cross before bolting up the staircase without another word. He had to put some separation between himself and the thing.

No, he thought. *I know what this beast is.*

His mind flashed to the open book as he ascended the steps higher and higher, every footfall sending a tinny reverberation around the empty chapel.

Clink, clink, clink.

Where is God, Father?

Again, the voice inside the old man's head scared him and caused goosebumps to break out all over his body.

"Get out of my head!" He'd reached the top of the steps now and stood with his hand clutching one of the small, sharpened crosses he'd made.

In silence, the old man stood, the only sound, his own ragged breathing. He had so many questions.

Why did such a creature exist to begin with?

Would God protect him?

And then the father felt a presence near him—he could hear another pair of lungs pulling the same air he breathed, but he couldn't move.

Fear held him in place as he asked one final question inside his mind.

Was God real at all?

The familiar, cunning voice of the creature—no, the *vampyre*—responded in his own head; it would be the last voice Father Gallagher would ever hear.

No.

The old man felt the push of the clawed hand on his chest before he saw the thing up close; what he saw was a man with cream-colored skin and deep blue eyes. Long fangs protruded from various places in his mouth, and his veins stood out in his neck, dark purple and prominent.

That was what the father was thinking of as his heart and spinal cord burst through the front of his chest after being impaled on the top of the cross.

It wasn't a deep thought, no profound realization, no revelation.

It was only death.

CHAPTER SIX

GEORGIA DAWSON AWOKE FROM a dream—no, a *nightmare*—with a short, startled scream. In the nightmare, she'd been hovering over her own bed, staring down at herself. She'd seen herself suffocating, the veins in her neck bulging out as she lay still, eyes wide-open and staring at the ceiling.

"Breathe!"

She'd screamed it over and over until she was as breathless as the dying avatar of herself on the bed.

In a haste, she'd waded across the room, each step a labor unto itself. She'd grabbed her own limp body and shaken it until the eyes locked onto hers.

The body on the bed grabbed Georgia's back and embraced her, her eyes panicked and frenzied.

"Just breathe!" she'd repeated.

She'd felt like she was drowning, watching herself struggle to remember how to draw breath. But now, she lay face down in a pool of sweat and drool. It was no wonder she couldn't breathe. She'd fallen asleep face down on her bedding.

"Ugh." She sat up slowly, her arms feeling weak as they struggled to hold up her weight.

She was most likely dehydrated. How long had it been since Mae had dropped her off? A quick glance over to the window showed it was still dark, so it likely hadn't been more than a couple of hours.

The nightmare crossed her mind, and she shuddered. She took a deep breath and let it out slowly. Anxiety and panic attacks weren't uncommon for Georgia, and the alcohol didn't help—as much as one would think it would.

If anything, she should be thankful to be alive. She'd heard stories of poor saps falling asleep—too drunk to function, only to choke to death on their own vomit in the night. The thought made her skin crawl.

Slowly, she swung her legs over the side of the bed and sighed as her feet hit the floor. A familiar feeling crept over her as she attempted to stand. Waves of nausea washed over her as she struggled to stop her body from swaying.

Still drunk.

If only that was all.

No, there was something on her mind, too—or rather, some*one.*

Georgia placed both hands on the bed and pushed herself up until she stood, swaying in the darkness of her bedroom, feeling silly. She'd been planning to confess her love for Mae Phillips tonight but had chickened out at the last moment.

It was something she'd been worrying over for years now. She knew Mae was married, and that it wasn't allowed for a woman to love another woman in that way, but she was tired of suppressing the feelings. It would have to be out in the open, even if that meant squashing the idea forever.

It was something she'd have to live with, one way or the other. But for now, she desperately needed to urinate.

She grabbed a candle from her nightstand and fumbled with a box of matches before striking one and lighting the small wick. The flame's glow lit the small room dimly and Georgia began making her way toward the bedroom door while still using one hand to steady herself along the wall. Already, a splitting migraine was setting in, and she knew she'd regret those last few drinks in the morning.

Georgia reached out with her free hand and gingerly opened the bedroom door. She peeked out into the dark hallway, something she had done since she was a small girl. Living alone as a single woman in Fort Whipple was seen as strange, but nobody could know how lonely it was.

Again, she thought of Mae, of how she wanted to hold her, to tell her everything. Hell, right now she was drunk enough to kiss her on the mouth.

Stop it. It won't—no, can't happen and you know it.

Georgia shook her head gently and blinked a few times in rapid succession. The longer she stood, the more the liquor seemed to have an effect on her—she found it difficult to simply keep her eyes open. But there was that aching urge again, and she was thankful to see the washroom door just down the hall.

Now she only had to take the first step.

And the next...

This was far from the first time she'd been in such a state—miserable and remorseful, maybe even a tad suicidal.

Surely it wouldn't be the last, either.

She reached the door to the washroom. Reaching out a shaky hand, she pulled the door open. She set the candle on the small counter and sat down to relieve herself.

Thank God for Lucille and Hank, she thought. They'd helped her install one of the town's first indoor toilets.

It's dangerous outside at night for a single lady.

Georgia had to place her hands on her knees to feel grounded, as if she'd float up through the ceiling if she didn't anchor herself to something.

A small sliver of moonlight shone on the floor in front of Georgia's feet. She glanced up through the tiny window above the sink and saw nothing but a thick blanket of black.

She'd finished urinating moments earlier but had yet to find the will to stand and make the journey back to bed. The whole room seemed to morph around her, and she could feel cool sweat collecting on her forehead.

Never again.

It also wasn't the first time she'd made *that* promise to herself.

Sudden, hostile shouting from outside startled Georgia out of her daze. She pulled herself to her feet, feeling a constricting fear grip her—threatening to shut down her heart and end it all.

Stay calm. It's just some drunk folks making fools of themselves.

She stumbled to the sink and turned on the water, cupping some of it in her hands to wet her face. She blinked and wiped her face dry and grabbed a small stool from under the sink. Even on the stool, she had to stand on her tiptoes to see out the window.

A small crowd, complete with lit torches, had amassed and the shouting had grown louder. Georgia was unable to make out any of their faces.

What in the world is going on?

Slowly, and as steadily as possible, she worked her way down off the stool, deciding to go outside and find out what the commotion was all about. The trip down the hallway was much quicker this time, but Georgia still stumbled and nearly hit her face on the bedroom doorframe. She sighed and quickly threw together a ramshackle outfit from clothes that had accumulated on the back of a tall, vertical mirror in the corner.

After dressing hastily, she slipped on an old pair of shoes and crossed the house to the front door. She swung open the old wooden door with a loud *WHAP* as it smacked against the wall behind it, flung open by a strong gust of wind.

Georgia had expected a crowd, but the gathering of shouting people was nowhere to be seen. She shook her head again, slowly this time, to avoid feeling too sick. She hadn't imagined the shouts, hadn't imagined the torches and the large crowd, had she?

She began walking in the direction she'd seen the crowd moving, a little scared but mostly drunk. There wasn't much in the way of reason moving her forward, just a strange curiosity to keep her feet moving.

Some of the houses were completely dark, wrapped in shadow while its occupants slept soundly. But there were a surprising number of houses with lights on. Some with the front door of the house ajar, as if the homeowners had left in a hurry.

One of those houses belonged to Hank and Lucille Hawthorne.

I'll get Lucille. She and Hank will know what to do.

It was tempting to go to Mae, now more than ever. But she didn't want to disturb her. Didn't want her to think any less of her.

She stumbled through the Hawthorne's open doorway and entered the small, dark house. It was terribly quiet inside and Georgia wondered if the Hawthorne's had been part of the mob she'd seen outside the window.

"Hello?" She tripped over a pair of shoes and cursed. She only barely caught herself from slamming her face into the kitchen wall. "Lucille? It's Georgia."

The house was dead-silent. Georgia's instincts were telling her to call out again, but she thought better of it.

What if Hank wakes up completely disoriented and attacks me?

She decided to make her way toward the bedroom, steadying herself along the hallway walls in the hopes of avoiding another accident. The liquor hadn't been kind to her, after all.

When she reached the Hawthorne's bedroom, she found the door partly open. Georgia peeked in and saw their silent shapes resting in their bed. She let out a small sigh of relief.

What am I doing?

She felt stupid for thinking this was a good idea—what if Lucille got angry with her? What if she called her a pathetic fucking drunk and told her to get the hell out of her house?

Georgia shook her head.

No, she decided. *I'm here now.*

She propped open the door a little wider and ambled slowly over to Lucille's side of the bed, much like she'd done plenty of times before as a small girl—only that had been her parent's bedroom, and only if she'd had a particularly frightening nightmare.

"Lucille..." Georgia began in a hushed whisper. She hung her head. "I'm tired of being alone."

She thought of Mae again, of how she wanted to spend her nights next to her, without a care in the world.

Georgia gingerly sat on the edge of the bed. "I just..." she continued, her voice a little louder now. "I think I'm in love with Mae, Lucille." She wiped a tear away from her face. "There, I said it!" Her words were slurred, but she didn't care. It felt amazing to get it off her chest—to tell another human being how she really felt.

"Lucille?" Georgia felt her friend's leg. It was cold to the touch.

Cold and *shriveled*.

Georgia scrambled to her feet. She felt around in the dark for a lantern and lit it, letting out a shrill, bloodcurdling scream as she saw the scene before her.

"Thank you all for coming." Sheriff Creighton stared out at the crowd that had gathered in the town hall. There was anger on their faces. Anger, but also sadness and confusion.

And fear.

"What in the Sam Hill is going on?" someone shouted from the back.

"We want answers!" another said.

Creighton took a slow, deep breath. Whether he liked it or not, this was part of the job. He knew that, but still, it didn't do much to make it any easier. The truth was that humans were weak creatures who could only pretend to be tough at best. Everyone wanted a leader—someone to look at when things got too hard, too confusing.

The people of Fort Whipple didn't seem to realize Creighton was human, too.

They also hadn't seen the *evil* he'd laid eyes upon as of late. How could he tell them?

He glanced at Buck Phillips, who wept silently near the back of the room. The man had witnessed true evil—true *terror*—had seen his wife, the love of his life, shriveled and dead. Her once-beautiful body was now a dried, rotten corpse.

He had seen all of this, and now he wanted revenge.

It was understandable. Creighton also wanted justice for Mae, for Geraldine Mayberry, and any other victims they were yet unaware of.

Ambrose stood to the sheriff's right, propped against the wall, his arms folded.

We could just as easily be mourning him right now.

And where would Creighton be if Ambrose had been among those slaughtered by this vile......*thing?*

He glanced back to Buck Phillips, who was crying louder now.

I wouldn't even be allowed to grieve. I'd still be expected to lead. Because that's what I do.

"Sheriff? Are you listening?"

Creighton shook his head. "As I was saying, thank you all for coming." He glanced around the room. All eyes were on him, all wanting *answers*. He took another deep breath and continued, "As you all know, there is a killer on the loose in Fort Whipple. Whoever..." He paused. "Or *what*ever it is, has been slaughtering livestock outside of town for some time now, and has now moved on to killing our friends, our family members, our neighbors."

The room was nearly silent now as every person waited for the plan of action.

"It's a demon, that's what it is!" shouted a drunk man from near the front of the room. "Fort Whipple is paying for its sins is all."

Creighton didn't know what to say. He'd seen the damned thing with his own eyes, whether he liked to admit it—he saw the thing's cold, dead eyes.

Its wings.

"Maybe it is," Creighton blurted, noting the gasps around the room. "And maybe we are. Who's to say?"

Creighton cared nothing for their shocked indignation. They hadn't seen what he'd seen. They didn't know what he knew.

He didn't know how to feel about anything anymore.

The chatter in the room grew louder.

What's it going to be, Sheriff?

The voice seemed to come from somewhere deep inside Creighton's very *being*.

A chill ran down his spine.

This won't end the way you think it will.

Creighton glanced around at all the faces. Before, he'd seen fear. He'd seen anger and confusion. Now, the faces all seemed to mock him.

A laugh erupted in Creighton's mind, causing him to jump just as the doors at the end of the room burst open.

What followed was a panic unlike Creighton had ever witnessed.

Standing in the open doorway was the very beautiful—very *drunk*—southern belle, Georgia Dawson. Hair plastered to her forehead with what looked like dried blood, she swayed in the open doorway, cradling a shotgun like a newborn.

Dark stains covered the front of Georgia's nightgown. But more concerning than her dress, to Creighton, was the look in the young woman's eyes.

That look would haunt Creighton.

"They're all dead," Georgia muttered, barely audible over the gasps and screams from around the room.

"*Mae* is dead." Georgia turned her head slowly to face Buck Phillips, who stood near the back of the room, his hand thumbing his holster.

Georgia turned to face Buck, swinging the shotgun up.

"No!" Creighton shouted, running toward Georgia.

This can't be happening.

"Georgia," Creighton said, standing in the center aisle, pistol aimed and ready. "You don't want to do this."

Ignoring the sheriff, Georgia repeated, "Mae is dead." She spit toward the grieving man. "And where the *fuck* were you?"

Creighton cocked his pistol. There was no part of him that wanted to shoot any citizen of Fort Whipple, especially someone dealing with such a terrible loss. But he couldn't back down. He had to stay strong.

"I'm warning you, goddamnit."

I'm going to have to kill her before she...

Pow.

Creighton had frozen just long enough for Georgia to turn the gun on herself. The sheriff felt as if he'd escaped reality and drifted into some sort of strange nightmare world. Oblivious to the shouts and wails around him, he wiped away the blood that had splattered his face and reached down, picking up the shotgun and cocking it. He handed the gun to a young man standing nearby.

In a quiet voice, he addressed the room. "All able-bodied men and women who want to help fight this thing—whatever it is—I suggest you take up arms and come with me."

CHAPTER SEVEN

THE NIGHT DRONED ON slowly as Freeman crouched low among a patch of brush near the town chapel. Already he could hear the familiar drone of flies humming over a fresh kill.

The sound of death.

He took a deep breath and shook his head, letting out a slow sigh.

"It wasn't meant to happen like this," he whispered to no one.

The Order was a sacred institution; it was only their unflinching adherence to laws and creeds long since written that kept them in good standing with humanity.

It meant they would be allowed to live.

Not exactly the right word for it.

Freeman had heard chatter from various members of The Order—the talk of rebellion. There were those who didn't care much for humans. Especially those humans who would dare give them an order. Such ways of thinking rarely ended well for young members of The Order. These rebellious youngsters often found an untimely demise—possibly their head on a stake or a public hanging.

But sometimes...

Freeman hung his head, clutching a handful of dirt, letting it slowly sift between his fingers.

Sometimes it's me who spills their blood.

"No matter."

Freeman had been quietly making his way toward the chapel when he'd seen the crowd of humans storming the streets. They were in some sort of assembly now, no doubt planning their defensive assault. He'd seen it before, many times—a small town trying its hardest to defend against a youth in their *blood frenzy*.

If only they knew they wouldn't stand a chance if they had all the guns in the world.

That's why I'm here.

"I know where you are, Jace," he whispered as he slinked along the backside of the chapel. He knew in the same way he knew how to breathe. Most likely it was a biological advantage—the ability to *sense* when potential prey is nearby.

Freeman could practically smell the priest's terror on the wind.

No.

Looking up, Freeman saw a small window, and with as much energy as he could muster, he scaled the wall and burst through, landing on the chapel floor in a burst of tiny glass shards.

Immediately, he was hit with the overpowering aroma of death.

Death, but mostly *blood*.

So much blood.

In the center of the room was a grotesque display unlike anything Freeman had seen in all his years. He could only stand in horrified awe of what Jace had done.

The humans will never forgive us.

"JACE!" Freeman roared. *"YOU MUST STOP THIS NOW!"*

But Jace wasn't listening. He was *feeding*.

In the center of the chapel, the priest lay impaled on the cross, his arms and legs splayed and dangling freely. Freeman could hear the quiet moans escaping the man's blood-soaked mouth.

Just death rattles, nothing more.

Freeman hoped.

The sight of the blood-soaked, gore-covered cross sent a shiver down Freeman's spine. But what struck him more than anything was the way Jace was feeding on the poor priest. At first, he appeared to have climbed up the cross for easy access to the throat, but now Freeman could see Jace was *floating* more than a dozen feet in the air.

His power has doubled, at least.

It was the worst Freeman could hope for. The *blood frenzy* was furious in Jace, unlike Freeman had ever seen.

The young vampyre turned his head and asked, "Care to join me?"

Freeman had to fight to keep his hands from shaking. Jace had the upper hand here—and he knew it. He was younger, stronger, faster.

He was devoid of empathy.

Still, Freeman was here to stop Jace by any means necessary, and he didn't take that directive lightly. Clenching his hands, he stood his ground. "You need to leave this place now. Flee and never turn back. It's the only way you'll survive."

"Survive?" Jace scoffed, nearly doubling over in laughter before swiftly flying through the air until he was mere inches from Freeman's face. "Is that what you call what we do?"

Freeman could smell the intoxicating aroma of a fresh human kill on Jace's breath. He sighed and did his best to maintain his composure—even after all these years, it still got to him.

Jace stepped even closer, and Freeman found himself mesmerized by the young vampyre's eyes. Was there something in them he'd seen before? Possibly in himself? Jace continued, "I didn't think so. I think you've been dead inside longer than I've been alive. That's what I think." He wiped at his mouth with the back of his sleeve. "Sorry about that," he added. "I'm a messy eater."

Freeman took his opportunity and struck as hard as he could at Jace's stomach, but Jace was faster. He grabbed Freeman's arm and flung him backwards with brute force, sending him crashing into an old piano behind him, ivory keys flying in all directions. Freeman watched as the dust from the piano rushed into the air and began to settle all around him.

That's all we are.

Dust.

He thought of The Order again. What would they think of him if they saw him now, weak and near-broken?

The Order doesn't care about you, that's why they sent you to die.

This wasn't Freeman's internal monologue. It was a message, a *whisper* into his mind.

He can hear my thoughts.

It was one of the reasons Jace had the upper hand—he knew Freeman's every move before he made it. Freeman's eyes drifted to the grim scene on the cross.

The priest didn't want to die. He'd been forced to jump, possibly even *pushed.*

A chill ran down Freeman's spine, and for the first time in all of his years working for The Order, he was genuinely *afraid.* His voice trembled when he spoke. "What you're doing is *wrong,* Jace. It's against everything The Order stands for. I'm trying to—"

"Fuck The Order!" Jace roared, his voice closer now as Freeman scrambled to his feet. "I don't subscribe to their new-age notions of *peace* with the humans. The universe never cared for me. Why should I go out of my way to appease those lesser than myself?"

Freeman stood on unsteady legs and pointed a finger at Jace. "You don't know what you're talking about. Without the treaty, the humans would have wiped us out already. Plain and simple. I *know* what you're going through, and this is never the answer."

Jace slowly levitated across the room toward Freeman. "Then why haven't they stopped me yet?" He let out a short bark of a laugh. "Stop living in fear, old man. They're powerless to stop us. Their blood gives us *strength.* It gives us *life.* Why do we deserve any less moral consideration?"

Freeman closed his eyes, took a deep breath. "These are people with emotions, Jace. With fears, aspirations, and families to look after. Who are you to destroy that?"

Jace shook his head. "Life is fueled by death, always. Do you mean to tell me all those cattle you slaughtered died willingly?" He scoffed. "I don't think so."

"These people aren't cows!" Freeman shouted. He was nearly face-to-face with Jace now.

Jace smiled. "Is that so? Tell me, what is it they do here in this forgettable little town that's so important? From what I can tell, all they do is eat, drink, and conspire against *niggers* like you."

Freeman knew it was true. It was one of the reasons he snuck around late at night. It wasn't exactly easy to blend in around Fort Whipple. But that was anywhere these days, especially in the South. Still, it wasn't any reason to *slaughter* these poor people. They were weak and simple, but most members of The Order had once been much the same.

Before *the change.*

The two of them were face-to-face now, and Freeman felt *weak.* He stared into Jace's eyes for a moment before a sense of overwhelming dread took over his whole being. He tried to shake it off, but there was something there... a sense of familiarity he couldn't explain, like a long-lost friend he'd once known. "I'm only going to tell you this last time to leave this place, Jace."

The young vampyre's face slowly morphed into a grotesque, insidious grin; and without speaking a word, his eyes drifted to the wall behind Freeman. "What do you think they'll do to you?" Jace asked, as Freeman turned to admire his work.

On the wall, written in the priest's blood, were three words: WHERE WAS GOD?

The message loomed over the chapel, a question with no answer.

Freeman jumped as he heard a loud *bang* on the chapel's front doors. He turned his head and was unsurprised to see Jace was nowhere to be found.

He planned this, the son of a bitch.

After a few moments, there had been rapping and slamming on the door, and Freeman stood there, frozen, as the doors opened wide and he stood before the angry mob—the unsettling scene behind him.

A moment of strained silence filled the air before their voices raised high, right along with their weapons.

Freeman held his hands just as high as his head hung low.

CHAPTER EIGHT

BUCK PHILLIPS STOOD WITH his shotgun aimed directly at the killer's face. The tall nigger stood with his hands high, not saying a word. Behind him, Father Gallagher lay splayed on the cross like a pig on a roasting spit.

"Lynch the motherfucker!" someone shouted from behind Buck.

Buck stood shoulder-to-shoulder with Sheriff Creighton—a man he'd known nearly all his life.

A man he respected.

But still, no amount of respect for a man's position would stop him from taking care of business. Law or no law, justice would be served tonight.

"I know what you're thinking, Buck," Creighton said in a low, shaky voice. "But we can't just kill this man here in cold blood." He turned to face his distraught friend. "He deserves a proper trial, just like anyone else. You know that."

No surprise. Creighton liked to play by the rules.

"You said it yourself back there, Sheriff. This ain't no normal man. He's a *monster.*"

Cheers and shouts of agreement erupted all around them.

Buck glanced up at the man in black who stood with his hands held high. Even from back here, he could tell there was something *different* about him—aside from the obvious—it was something in the eyes, Buck figured.

Lifeless.

"He's a killer if I've ever seen one, Creighton." Buck gripped the holster at his waist and unsheathed a large hunting knife. He looked deep into the sheriff's eyes with an expression of a man suffering something between insanity and insomnia. "He killed *Mae*. He doesn't get to live." He pointed a trembling finger in the sheriff's face. "I'm gonna kill this dumb sumbitch, and *you* won't do a goddamn thing to stop me."

The sheriff didn't reply. He only stood staring at the words scrawled in blood.

"My god..." Creighton said, seemingly unaware of Buck's presence.

"He doesn't have the stones!" came a voice from the back of the crowd. More shouts of protest and anger followed as Fort Whipple's finest stood idle.

Without another word, Buck joined the mob as they stormed further into the chapel. The coppery tang of blood mixed in the air with a scent which reminded Buck of hunting with his father as a child. It was the unpleasant aroma of a butchered animal, its guts on the outside of its body—only this time it was the priest whose body lay on display for all to see.

"You stay right there, boy," Buck growled.

The black man stood still as a statue, and for the first time, he spoke. "I'm here to help stop this. To help *all* of you."

"Bullshit!" Buck roared. "We caught you red-handed. We know what you done here, and we're going to see to it that you don't live to see morning."

The black man's face slowly morphed into a delicate grin. "I appreciate your vigor, friend. But I'm telling you, you've got the wrong—"

His words were cut off as a man from the crowd slammed him in the mouth with a quick right hook.

The black man barely flinched.

Wiped that ugly smile off the bastard's face, I did.

Buck looked back over his shoulder to see the sheriff slowly approaching the mob. He took his chance and joined in as more and more fists and weapons rained in on the murderous stranger.

Each impact of Buck's now-bloodied fists did little to ease his pain.

And still, as the crowd descended on the black man, he did nothing to defend himself against their blows; he simply stood there and took the beating.

Buck paused for a moment, watching as Agnes Willow struck the man with a broom handle.

There was something in the man's eyes—which Buck noted were a cold blue—a spark of something. It was almost as if the man were speaking directly into his mind.

I didn't do this.

Creighton stood ashamed and shocked at his own inaction as the citizens of Fort Whipple lynched a man right in front of him.

It seemed a switch had flipped inside of Creighton sometime in the past twenty-four hours or so. No amount of training or experience could have prepared him for this.

His eyes drifted up to the murdered priest, but only for a split-second—it was all he could stomach. He turned away in disgust, retching and holding his hand over his mouth.

Why did this happen?

How?

Could the priest have jumped? Inflicted this horrible demise upon himself? Creighton didn't think so.

Still, the black man standing before the angry mob was certainly *not* the creature he and Ambrose had encountered. Even so, he was a stranger in town and he needed a proper questioning and trial, just like anyone else.

Buck Phillips be damned.

And like a ghost of a long-forgotten memory, Ambrose pushed his way through the crowd toward him, shouting, "That's not him, Daddy!"

Creighton knew that. Or, to be more specific, he was about ninety percent certain it was the truth.

Over the roar of the crowd, Creighton could hear the stranger calmly and plainly stating that he was innocent—that he had actually come to help stop the actual killer.

What is your role in this scenario, Sheriff?

Creighton twitched. A chill reverberated through his body. It was a sort of tick he'd had since childhood—any time he got too excited or nervous about something, he'd sort of *tweak* a bit.

Right now, his blood ran cold—the question that bore its way into his head wasn't from his own mind. Creighton knew that, and still...

There was a curious desire to *talk back*.

"Ambrose, you shouldn't be here. Too dangerous."

Ambrose weaved awkwardly between two drunks brandishing lit torches. "To hell with that." His hand went down to where his holstered pistol rested. "I aim to finish the job." He pointed at the man at the front of the room, raising his voice to be heard over the jeers and boos around the room. "But that's not the thing that attacked me. That's ain't what's been haunting this town."

Creighton nodded, amazed at how grown Ambrose had become. "I know, Son."

"Then what are you doing?"

Nothing. You'll do nothing, just like always.

Creighton stumbled backwards a bit, as if hit by a blow to the stomach.

If you killed yourself, the worms would rejoice.

He gasped.

The rest of the world would feel nothing.

"Daddy!"

The loud *whap* of fist against flesh snapped Creighton back to the present. The assault on the strange man had begun.

Creighton looked at Ambrose with an intensity behind his eyes. "If things go south, you fire that pistol of yours in the air, you hear me?"

"Yessir."

The sheriff pushed his way to the front of the crowd, holding his gun high. "This ends, now!"

"Now he wants to do his job," he heard someone shout.

Creighton shoved his way through the mob and emerged in just enough time to see Buck Phillips pull a large hunting knife out of his boot and hold it to the stranger's throat.

"I oughta kill you right this fuckin' instant."

Creighton aimed his revolver. "Be the last thing you do, Buck. Think about that. Now I want order, goddamnit. And right fucking now."

Gasps erupted around the room. Creighton could see Ambrose getting a good vantage point from the other side of the room should the crowd turn on him.

Yes. He's a smart boy.

Did you know he shot me in the face?

Creighton wanted to scream. It took everything in him to hold his composure as he aimed the gun at Buck Phillips—who showed no signs of backing down.

I will make him pay for that.

I will make you pay as well.

"MAKE IT STOP!" Creighton shrieked at the top of his lungs, scaring Buck Phillips so badly that he dropped his knife and backed away from the black man with his hands up.

"Fine, Sheriff. If that's how it's going to be, put the goddamned greasy nigger on trial for all I care. Hell, maybe you can have him over to fuck your wife first?"

Creighton leveled his revolver between Buck's beady eyes. "One. More. Word."

Pull the trigger. He's not worth the oxygen he consumes.

What's more, he wants you to do it.

Creighton's hand shook as his finger wavered near the trigger. He felt like a man watching through someone else's eyes—completely unable to control his actions, his thoughts.

It was a strange hell.

Creighton had to reach deep down within to fight the alien feeling. He glanced up once more to the cross, but there were no answers there.

Only pain.

Buck's eyes held nothing but genuine, unwavering fear. His stringy brown hair matted to his forehead—his breathing shaky. He reminded Creighton of a raccoon caught in a bear trap.

"You really going to kill me, Tom?"

Of course you are, the miserable thing has nothing to live for, anyway.

Creighton lowered his gun. "Help me get him down to the jailhouse." He moved toward him until he was close enough to smell Buck's dinner. "And don't *fuck with me.*"

A long pause filled the room with silent anticipation. The shock and disappointment of the angry mob was a palpable feeling that threatened to weigh on Creighton's mind, but only for a moment.

The law was the law—no matter how these people felt about it. He turned and pulled his handcuffs from his belt, facing the stranger. "This is only a precaution, friend."

The black man nodded. "I understand your position here, Sheriff, and I thank you."

"Friend, he says," hissed someone from behind Creighton.

And then that distant, dark voice whispered once more inside the sheriff's mind.

Are you sure you don't want to kill him, just to be sure?

Creighton shook his head, as if he could shake the thoughts out of his ears. The thought crossed his mind—only for a moment—that the crowd must surely think he was losing his mind.

How can you be so sure you aren't?

"I can't..." Creighton muttered as he tightened the handcuffs around the man's dark wrists. He noticed a flicker of something in the stranger's eyes at that and immediately wished he hadn't spoken.

"You can call me Freeman."

Creighton stared at the man, nodded. He turned his gaze to where Ambrose stood, still ready with his.22, and waved his hand for him to follow.

Turning back to Freeman, he said, "Let's get you down there before this gets worse."

Freeman had watched the sheriff from afar, but it wasn't until now that he *knew* him. In the same way, he knew his victims of old—intimately.

The sheriff's character was on full display. Even amidst dreadful fear and uncertainty, he did the right thing.

Presently, he led Freeman and the boy, Ambrose, through the crowd, shouldering his way past men much bigger than himself. Freeman could feel their hatred emanating from them like warmth off a fresh kill.

He dodged out of the way as a volley of spit came toward his face.

The boy shouted from behind Freeman. "You watch yourself, mister."

As calm as the sheriff seemed on the outside, he was petrified. Freeman could sense his fear. He didn't blame him. The townsfolk wanted blood, and he was the only thing between them and what they would consider sweet, sweet revenge.

They want blood.

Freeman had to stifle a chuckle.

The four of them made their way out of the church—Buck Phillips included. It was Freeman's understanding that he was the jailor, after all.

The boos and jeers of the mob could be heard echoing in the night air, even when they were well down the street from the chapel. The wind whipped around them and it felt good on Freeman's bruised face. He began to wonder what would happen next. He wasn't strong enough in the power of suggestion to convince the sheriff to let him walk—at least not right away.

With Jace running free, every minute is crucial.

He knew he could most likely overpower the small group. The handcuffs would prove to be of little concern. But still...whatever foresight Freeman liked to think he had was screaming at him to remain peaceful.

For now.

"Here we are," Creighton announced.

Freeman knew the jailhouse. He'd observed it from afar for sometime, much like most of the town of Fort Whipple. It was Freeman's favorite part of the job—he never knew where he'd be traveling next.

He enjoyed watching people. Not in a predatory way. No, he'd long since put those desires to rest. The Order had, of course, demanded it. But with a little teaching and dedication to their master plan, he'd come around to see things their way. It was something he prided himself in—the ability to still empathize with humanity.

Amazing, really, how quickly one forgets.

Freeman ducked as he entered the small jailhouse doorway, followed closely by the punch-drunk jailor.

Buck grabbed Freeman's arm and half-spun him to face him. "I hope you enjoy sleeping on the floor with the rats, you greasy, black mother—"

"Goddamn you, Buck, that's enough of your horse-shit tonight!" Creighton bellowed. "The man ain't done a thing, far as we know. So how about you get him in the cell for questioning, and shut your fuckin' hole for once?"

Freeman winced. He felt sorry for the jailor, having lost his wife in such a way—to have *found* her in such a state...

A quick glance around the suddenly near-silent room showed the sheriff didn't seem too proud of himself.

Creighton took off his hat and hung it on a hook by the doorway. "Listen, Buck, it's been a long night. And I'm sorry about Mae. I really am. But you're seeing red right now."

Buck shook his head and let out a short laugh. "It ain't red I'm seeing." He turned to face Freeman and seemed to think better of finishing the thought.

Oh, how quickly I could drain your entire body of your precious life force.

Freeman shook his head. Those thoughts still came from time to time—it was the self-discipline to bury them deep within that made The Order as special as it was. Certainly there was a dignity about it that a man such as *Buck Phillips*—with the intellectual capacity of a trained circus animal—could never begin to comprehend.

Freeman turned his attention to the kind sheriff. "Sir, is it really necessary to keep me overnight? I have come here only to help your people. Of this you *must* trust me."

Buck made a sound with his mouth, which sounded close to a horse's chuffing, but quickly stopped when he caught the sheriff's glare.

"Tell you what," Sheriff Creighton said. "How about you make yourself useful? Go get me a drink. Get yourself one too, hell." He turned to face Freeman. "And what about you, friend? Would you join us?"

Buck looked perplexed, as if he were searching for the right words to say but was born mute.

"None for me, thanks." And as Buck shuffled away toward the liquor cabinet in the corner, Freeman took his chance. "Again, do you really have to lock me up?" He put as much attention in his *focus* as he could muster, but feared it wouldn't be enough.

"Daddy," Ambrose called from the window near the front door, "they're all out here, and they don't look happy."

Creighton didn't seem surprised in the least. "That's just the thing, Mr. Freeman. Putting you in that cell could be the best thing that happens to you this evening."

Freeman understood and appreciated the sentiment, sure. But the sheriff didn't know he had the ability to take down any man with ease, should he decide to.

Freeman sighed. "I know what is happening in this town. I've been camping in the desert for near a fortnight in anticipation of this...... he searched for the right word. *"Injustice."* His eyes searched the sheriff's for any sign of emotion one way or the other—for a human. He was incredibly difficult to read when he wanted to be. He added, "I only wish I'd caught him sooner."

"Friend of yours, then?"

Freeman shook his head. "It's complicated. All I can tell you is I can help you stop it for good."

Creighton paused, lips pursed as if daring to speak, but no sound came out.

Buck returned to the room with two near-full glasses of a dark brown liquid. Freeman barely remembered the taste of alcohol—it had been *so long*. It had never really been a vice of his, however. He guessed that was lucky for him.

"I may've got a little head start," Buck admitted, liquor strong on his breath and wetting his gray mustache. "Forgive me, it's been a horrific evening. I think we can all agree." He shot a piercing glare in Freeman's direction.

Freeman had lived his fair share of grief and loss. He well knew the heartache the old jailor was experiencing—the toll it takes on one's mental and physical health. Freeman was simply a simple target, a way of directing his pain.

He also knew of such common human emotional deficiencies. It was something that was slow to leave, even long after the last breath of life had evacuated one's lungs.

"Best we get you in a cell for now," Creighton said, turning toward Freeman. "No cuffs, though. And remember, it's for your protection at this point."

No. No. This is not what I need right now.

"—all for show, really," Creighton continued. "Let me address the town. Fort Whipple is in a downright panic, as you are well aware. Then we can get down to brass tacks."

Freeman nodded, catching Buck's toothy grin from behind the sheriff as he took another long pull of whiskey. The drunken man held up a hand and waved it slightly.

"This way." Creighton unlocked a small cell near the front desk and stepped aside, letting Freeman enter. The cell was small, around eight feet by six feet. Enough room only for a small cot.

I should be putting an end to Jace's reign of terror, but instead, I'm sitting in here like the town drunkard.

"Sheriff," he said, meeting Creighton's eyes with his own. "Please make haste. We have to stop him tonight."

Creighton paused for a moment, picking up his glass from the desk. He knocked it back swiftly, swallowing the drink in one swift gulp. "I hope you're right." He grabbed his keys from his belt and slipped a small silver key into the lock on Freeman's handcuffs.

It was a relief, having his hands free. Freeman rubbed his wrists absentmindedly and took a seat on the cot. As the sheriff locked the cell, a small chuckle could be heard from Buck, who currently had the whiskey bottle upended in his mouth. It was only after Creighton had made his way out the front door that Buck made the sound again and Freeman realized it hadn't been laughing at all.

Buck was sobbing. "I mean... I know she wasn't exactly faithful..."

He sniffled. "Fucking dead..." he slammed back another shot. Freeman would have liked to have told him to slow down, but he had a feeling he'd be passed out soon enough. The man looked like hell. Besides, he certainly wouldn't have any interest in anything Freeman had to say—especially with the sheriff gone outside to address the mob.

Cheers erupted outside as Creighton's voice grew louder, but it was impossible to discern what was being said. Freeman looked down at his dark hands. They'd begun to take on the harsh, shriveled appearance of one who is near-starved of blood.

The hunger is becoming unbearable.

The shuffling of feet across the wood floor snapped Freeman back to attention. He looked up to see Ambrose standing near the cell door. There was fear in the boy's eyes. But fear was not the only thing Freeman recognized in those eyes. There was also a stubborn determination and undying loyalty. The boy was a good soul—the type of human that made Freeman glad to take on his role with The Order.

"I know it wasn't you," the boy said. Strands of hair poked out from under his oversized cowboy hat. "I... I shot the thing that's been killing everyone. I saw it *up close.*" He gulped, lowering his voice. "It didn't even look human."

Jace had truly been terrorizing these people, flying about town, a fully animalistic, chaotic horror. He had been *feeding* on their families. It was no wonder they wanted him dead.

Freeman looked the boy in the eyes. "I know, son. My intention was to stop him tonight, to stop him from harming anyone else." His eyes went to the desk, where the keys lay on their large hoop-ring. Behind the desk, Buck was snoring.

"Do you believe me?" Freeman asked the boy.

"Yes."

"Do you want me to stop him?"

The boy nodded. "I want you to kill him."

Freeman winced. "Then you know what to do, son. Quickly, before he comes back!"

The boy understood. He turned and grabbed the keyring, careful not to let them make too much noise—though, Freeman figured a train could roll through the jailhouse right about then without waking the jailor.

"I don't know which key opens this cell," the boy said, handing the ring over to Freeman.

It was of no concern to Freeman. He'd locked the exact key in his memory when the sheriff had locked the cell. Gold with a chip near the base. He quickly located the key and faced the boy. "Listen, I'm going to need you to close your eyes. Just for an instant, and I'll be gone. Understand?"

The boy looked confused, but nodded.

"Now!"

The boy turned and squeezed his eyes tight, and Freeman unlocked the cell, and exploded from the room in a burst of leathery wings.

CHAPTER NINE

AMBROSE STOOD SHAKING SLIGHTLY as Buck Phillips snored away at the desk in the corner, his feet propped up, arms crossed over his chest. He couldn't seem to wrap his mind around what he'd just witnessed.

What *had* he witnessed?

There was a strange familiarity about the man... the *creature,* whatever it was. He was much like the other one—the *bad* one. The way he had *blasted* from the room. Flown?

Ambrose shook his head. Had he just let the wrong man go?

No. The other one seemed different. Younger. Lighter skin.

Still... the eyes were the same.

Outside, cheers erupted at something his daddy had said, and Ambrose suddenly realized his time was short before he'd have to explain what happened to their captive.

I hope I made the right decision.

Nothing could have prepared a child as young as him for this type of horror. Even his daddy—the sheriff of Fort Whipple, and a man highly respected for his courage and integrity—seemed as lost as Ambrose felt.

His hand went to his.22 on his belt. His fingers worked their way over the smooth metal and he unholstered it, feeling the weight of it between his fingers.

Who am I kidding?

He'd shot the monster right in the face and it hadn't seemed to slow it in the slightest. What was he going to do with a small varmint pistol?

Just piss the thing off more.

Ambrose sat down in a chair facing the door, still holding the gun in one hand. His mind drifted to the scene in the chapel. There had been that phrase written in blood...

Where was God?

"Maybe this is His plan," he muttered under his breath. "To let us all be picked off, one by one."

Buck snored again, louder this time, and a plot began to formulate in Ambrose's mind. He jumped to his feet quickly before he had time to second-guess himself—and before his daddy was done speaking to the townsfolk.

Buck was a large man, which was going to make this a difficult task, but Ambrose wasn't exactly a frail boy, either. He approached the jailor's ancient wooden desk and glanced down at the once-full whiskey bottle sitting there.

Nearly gone.

Ambrose didn't know much about liquor, but he knew enough to know Buck was basically dead, or as close to death as a living person could be. He could tell that just by *looking* at the man.

Truth be told, he felt great pity for Buck Phillips. Of the many lives lost in Fort Whipple, his wife Mae was among the most tragic. She'd been a good woman, and now the dirty old drunk had nobody.

Heart pounding hard in his chest, Ambrose decided it was now or never. He grabbed the back of the chair and gave it his all as he tried to drag it.

It barely budged, making a loud scraping noise across the rough wooden floor.

Ambrose sighed quietly. It turned out his plan wasn't going to work after all.

Have to hurry. He could come back in here any second.

Buck stirred then, yawned, but by all accounts still appeared very much asleep—even when he said, "Mae, s'that you?"

The boy's heart sank, but he saw his opportunity. Voice shaking, he tried his best falsetto, "Come on, Buck, let's get you to bed." It was all he had.

"What? Mmm......okay, sure." Buck grumbled, shooting up out of his chair and immediately collapsing, holding onto Ambrose for support.

"Come on, this way," Ambrose said.

Buck said nothing, only nodded. Luckily for Ambrose, he hadn't seemed to open his eyes the entire time. It was all the man could muster to be led somewhere like a blind man. His feet shuffled in heavy, sloshing steps.

Ambrose led Buck into the exact cell from which he'd just helped the black stranger escape. It seemed fitting, seeing the way he'd treated the man. The way he used that slave word against him made Ambrose feel uncomfortable. He couldn't imagine hating someone based only on their physical appearance, without knowing anything else about them. Even the natives still roaming the desert—Ambrose grimaced when he heard them called "savages" so freely and often.

"M'tired," Buck managed. His shin hit the side of the cot and he did a strange sort of swooping spin, landing hard on the bed—the springs making an awful wrenching sound.

It worked!

Ambrose could barely stop his hands from shaking as he slowly closed the cell and turned the key in the lock.

"What makes you think that black fella's innocent?" a small, wiry woman named Agnes Middleditch asked.

Creighton rubbed his tired eyes, sighed. He'd been answering the same questions again and again. Half the town was drunk, and everyone was exhausted.

Like wrangling a bunch of young'uns.

"Again, Miss Middleditch, I assure you we've been more than adequate in our precautions. We've got our man held for questioning, but I can't stress enough: the killer is still out there." Creighton raised his voice, forced some bite into his speech. "It's time we split into groups and find this son of a bitch. Anyone who isn't looking for conflict tonight needs to go home, lock their doors."

"Didn't help Mae Phillips," someone jeered from the back of the crowd.

"Miss Mayberry neither," another added.

Creighton felt like he was walking through quicksand with iron boots. There was no backup, no one to confide in. The weight on his shoulders was insurmountable. And all the while he had the thought in the back of his mind—though he tried to keep it at bay, little nips at the flask here and there—*Is Mary Ann okay?*

It had been at least a couple hours since he and Ambrose had left her all alone.

Fort Whipple isn't that big. If that thing isn't here...

Creighton shook his head, and for the second time in less than twenty-four hours he regretted the drink. It made him sluggish.

Weak.

Right now, he wanted a mug full of strong, black coffee.

He spoke with as much energy as he could muster: "Listen, anyone who's joining the hunt needs to group up amongst themselves. No more than four or five to a group. We'll all split up in different directions and shout like hell when we see something."

It wasn't much of a plan, but it was something. Sometimes, it was all the people needed—for someone they deem less weak than themselves to state the obvious.

It worked. Immediately, the townsfolk began congregating amongst themselves, dividing into groups.

Ambrose emerged from the front of the jailhouse, a panicked look in his eye. He panted, dropped to his knees. "It all happened so fast, Daddy," he said, a hitch in his voice. "I'm sorry I let you down." He hung his head and stared at the ancient wooden planks below.

Creighton glanced over his shoulder, noticed nobody had seemed to notice Ambrose, much less overheard what was said. He stepped closer to his son, reached down, and pulled him up by one arm. "What are you talking about, boy? What happened?"

"I had to take a leak," Ambrose said, leading the way inside the jailhouse. "I stepped out the backdoor for twenty seconds and I came back to this." He pointed at the cell where Buck lay snoring. The keys to the cell lay on top of Buck's protruding stomach.

"What the hell?" Creighton looked around the room, opening and closing doors, cursing. "Where is Freeman? How did this happen?"

Ambrose's eyes fell again to the floor. "I don't know, Daddy. I heard this... *noise*, and next thing I knew, something shot past me like a bullet. I'm surprised you didn't hear it."

Shot past me like a bullet. What does that mean?

Creighton shot a glance toward the near-empty whiskey bottle and grimaced.

"I heard them arguing," Ambrose offered. "Buck kept calling the other man... names. He was pretty drunk."

Creighton nodded, still not comprehending what had happened. But there was one thing he did know—Ambrose was hiding something. There was his classic tell—staring at the floor while speaking. Something else, though...something wasn't right.

Call it a hunch, but damn it, I know when my boy's lying to me.

"Well, it sure won't hurt for Buck to sleep it off in there. Maybe this Freeman fella put him in there for his own protection. Still, I sure wish we could have questioned him."

Ambrose said nothing.

"Are you sure you don't know anything about how he got out of the cell?"

Creighton's son seemed to think for a moment, a face the sheriff had seen many times before. It was the face of a smart young man working out a particularly difficult problem.

"All I know is that man says he came here to defend us." Each word was carefully chosen, and the sting of realization was not lost on Creighton.

Neither of them spoke for some time until Ambrose broke the silence with a question, a pained expression on his face. "What are they, Daddy?"

Creighton felt a chill ripple down his spine. Suddenly, it became clear in his mind—at least to some extent.

What they were dealing with wasn't human. More importantly, however, was the fact that there were two of them loose around town.

God, I hope Freeman was telling the truth about helping us.

"Daddy?"

"Your guess is as good as mine, son." Creighton whirled and faced the door. "Come on, we've got to find the... well, the bastard that's been terrorizing the town." He headed out of the jailhouse without another look back. Ambrose followed close behind.

Townsfolk huddled together in groups numbering anywhere from two to five. Creighton noticed some had left already—whether to go home and hide behind locked doors—of which he couldn't blame them, or to get an early start on the hunt.

Men and women alike stood with cocked shotguns, rifles, pistols, and various other weaponry—not excluding gardening tools and the like. Creighton even noticed someone who held a small wooden cross with the lowest tip sharpened to a fine, deadly point.

A grim image, Creighton mused. Especially considering the events of this evening.

Nervous energy filled the air, but the faces of the crowd told another story.

It was time.

"Alright, let's go! Remember, this thing is dangerous as hell. So if you see the cocksucker, it's shoot first, ask questions later."

"Oh, and make as much noise as you possibly can, so the rest of us know where to go. Understood?"

A cheer rose from the crowd, their fear and anger erupting over into ecstatic potential.

Creighton had to admit, he *wanted* to be the one to bring it to its knees. He wanted to make it pay for what it had done; the law be damned.

It had been that kind of evening.

CHAPTER TEN

FREEMAN STOOD ON THE outskirts of Fort Whipple, the wind whipping his cloak against blood-stained boots. He thought back to the poor cat he'd feasted on earlier in the evening.

That was how he felt now, like a feline licking his wounds.

There had been no sign of Jace since the scene at the church, and Freeman had begun to wonder if the *blood frenzy* was coming to an end.

Instinct told him otherwise. He imagined Jace was waiting somewhere, biding his time while the majority of the town gathered all together, just as he was.

Of course, another sickening thought filled Freeman's mind.

What if he's silently picking them off while they sleep in their beds?

Freeman let out a low chuckle. "Who's sleeping tonight?"

Fools and drunks.

He knew that's how Jace would think of the matter. Anyone stupid enough to let their guard down tonight—during such an event as his *frenzy*—deserves to die a fool's death.

It wasn't, of course, the way The Order looked at things, however...

But Jace had blasphemed The Order. He'd turned his back and gone well out of his way to make sure he'd never be accepted back, *blood frenzy* or not.

Freeman's fears had been realized. This can only end in death.

In pain.

Freeman's lips were cracked, his throat dry. His very bones felt weak. It had been too long since he'd had a decent feeding, and he felt nearly powerless against the much stronger vampyre. But it had to be done.

He had a plan, but he didn't know if he had the strength to go through with it.

Only one way to find out.

He thought of Mother Kynes—the way her long, black fingernails tapped against the mahogany table as her words echoed along the Great Hall back home:

End it quickly or end HIM.

The Order knew the threat was especially high—Jace being a particularly rebellious case.

Freeman hadn't spent much time with the boy previously, but his reputation was well known. Even before this murderous streak he'd shown... tendencies. Violence and anger seemed to follow him everywhere he went.

The wind picked up, and Freeman pulled his cloak up around his neck. It was time to move in and finish it. Jace needed to be stopped before he could destroy more lives in this poor town.

And the boy, Ambrose—Freeman was especially fond of that one. He'd shown him true kindness, even when it was the hardest thing he could've done. He reminded him of so many mentors he'd had in the past; the boy was special.

Movement stirred near the jailhouse, and Freeman could see the groups splitting off in different directions, torchlight marking their location.

Either they will find him, and the screams will make it obvious... or I'll find him first.

A terrible thought crept its way into Freeman's mind: *Or he will find them first.*

Freeman moved toward the outskirts of the town, near the back of the saloon. He kept low and moved quietly across the dusty ground. His head snapped to his right when he heard a faint rustling, but he found it was only a lone tumbleweed blowing in the wind among dry brush.

If only tumbleweeds could talk, Freeman mused. *Maybe it could point me in the right direction.*

Then came the scream, low at first—definitely male—then evolving into something completely different. The sound sent goosebumps across Freeman's flesh. His throat closed, his nerves on edge.

Animalistic shrieks were accompanied by the vicious tearing of flesh, reminding Freeman of an encounter he'd once had with a notoriously evil group—The JM Gang. They'd been hunted during another youth's *frenzy*. Freeman had never told a soul, but he'd waited until the whole group of them were good and dead before apprehending the young vampyre.

Freeman ran at full speed now, just barely missing the torchlight of one of the small search groups as he rounded the corner down the street to his left. The pained shrieks came from one of the townsfolk's backyards.

Freeman approached the back right corner of the house, peered around in anticipation. Immediately, his senses were overcome with the distinct head-rush that usually came with an immense amount of blood. His hand shook as he reached for his knife.

The screams had been replaced with dull, lifeless gurgles.

Freeman gasped in horror as he saw the figure on the ground, pulling itself along the dirt, leaving long streaks of his own blood behind him.

It was an elderly man, maybe seventy years old. Behind him, Jace stood with arms crossed as he watched the man struggle. A trail of blood and ragged skin followed behind the man, leading back to the broken window he'd been yanked from.

The man before Freeman was barely recognizable as human. In a matter of seconds, his humanity had been traded for a pulpy, red-and-purple abomination. He dragged himself along with a sad determination, as if there were any chance of survival. There was only one fate that awaited this poor soul.

Without another thought, Freeman approached the man, turned him over, and slipped his knife into his heart with as much force as he could manage. "I'm sorry," he whispered in a somber voice. "You didn't deserve this."

A loud *snap* let Freeman know Jace had taken this chance to escape. He turned to look and the other vampyre was gone. It seemed to be his motive—to get Freeman caught again.

I need more strength to fly.

He looked down at the poor dead man on the ground. His stomach lurched.

His eyes drifted to the moon, it seemed to taunt him. It was well on its way down near the crest of the earth; the sun threatening to peek out shortly.

Everything in him wanted to feast, to restore some of his strength. Logic told Freeman it was likely the only way he even stood a chance.

The only way the boy, Ambrose, stood a chance.

But... The Order.

The code.

Again, the memory of Mother Kynes: *End it or end HIM.* Her croaking, blood-starved voice echoed in his mind.

Presently, Freeman sighed. He knelt low and inspected the kill. There was no shortage of blood to be had. It wouldn't be hurting anyone to...

He heard footsteps getting closer and snapped his attention back to the task at hand. He had little time to waver on the decision now. Closing his eyes, he whispered quietly, "Forgive me."

His face and beard were quickly dyed a deep crimson as Freeman found a good vein. His eyes nearly rolled back in his head, and they, too, took on a crimson hue—his body having tasted its first fill of human blood in years.

Decades.

Freeman's guilt was rapidly replaced with invigorating bloodlust. His strength was immense, each muscle in his body rippled with renewed vitality. It felt like he could take on the world.

His heightened senses told him he had mere seconds before he was discovered feasting on the remains of someone's neighbor.

It ends now.

Freeman planted his hands in the bloodstained dirt and, with concentrated effort, sprouted massive bat-like wings and kicked off from the ground with such force that he soared into the night sky—just as the horrified screams and shouts for help filled the air.

Freeman's clothes were essentially destroyed, but that couldn't bother him now. He floated high over Fort Whipple, searching for Jace like a hawk in pursuit of a rabbit.

"I'm a god," he whispered to no one.

"I'm the god of broken dreams and premature death. Hear me coming and fear me, but know that I cannot be stopped."

What am I saying?

Freeman's mind raced. Each sensation was amplified. Every breath had its own rhythm, its own cadence. Each exhalation, a beautiful staccato masterpiece reverberating in his head. He'd never felt such feelings in all his many years.

"This is what The Order is afraid of," Freeman mused. His eyes had gone fully blood-red.

I'm the predator now, Jace.

I'm the killer who comes in the night.

And I will end you.

CHAPTER ELEVEN

AMBROSE CREIGHTON WATCHED WITH pride as his daddy did what he did best—calm and support the people of Fort Whipple. He wasn't sure if they'd find the *creature*. *Maybe* it had long since left, flown off into the mountains to terrorize some native tribe.

Possibly, it was hiding around the nearest corner, waiting to rip Ambrose's head from his body. He shivered, looked off to the mountains in the distance, and wished he were anywhere else.

Sheriff Creighton turned to face his son as the crowd dispersed through the dark streets, torches at the ready.

"Son, come here." He bent over, got eye-to-eye with him. "It's best if we keep it quiet about our guest escaping. Buck will sleep it off just fine in there." He sighed. "Everyone seemed ready. Capable. I feel like that knowledge would only deflate them."

"I know." It was all Ambrose could think to say. He knew his daddy knew he'd let the prisoner escape, and it almost bothered him that he hadn't mentioned it.

Unless it was a relief for him.

"Which way are we going, Daddy?" Ambrose wasn't afraid of the monster. He'd already shot it once and would have no problem doing so again.

His daddy frowned. "That's just it, son." He straightened, stood. "Now, I know you want to come with me and kill this *boogeyman*, but you've got your mama sittin' at home alone while that monster slowly picks off the town."

Ambrose's hand drifted to the handle of his .22 pistol.

"Do you understand what I'm saying?" There was desperation in his daddy's eyes. It was an expression Ambrose had never seen before. Something between shock and exhaustion.

He nodded. "Yessir." He tried to hide the fear in his voice.

Ambrose wasn't scared of walking home alone. He was nervous about what he might find when he got there. It wasn't like he hadn't thought of it already—of course his mama had crossed his mind. But she wasn't exactly helpless, either.

That's right. She knows where the shotgun is.
She knows how to use it.

"Ambrose?"

He turned to face his daddy, his face solemn.

"It's time to be a man now."

Ambrose nodded. "Yessir."

Creighton watched as his son took off in the direction of their home. He wasn't a religious man, not truly—deep down—but he said a little prayer, anyway.

Certainly can't hurt at a time like this.

He unholstered his pistol and counted his bullets for what felt like the tenth time tonight—though there was this nagging part that reminded him:

Guns could be completely useless against it.

Ambrose had shot the creature in the face and it hadn't even slowed it down.

He shook his head, sighed. *And I'm sending him away to defend his mama with nothing more than a little rat pistol.*

Then came that intrusive, snake-like voice. It pried its way into the forefront of Creighton's thoughts with a primal intensity:

Why stand around, Sheriff? Don't you have a bad guy to catch?

Creighton didn't need to guess who the voice belonged to. It was the creature, the one the black man—Freeman—had called *Jace.*

What do you do, Creighton wondered, *when you can't even control your own thoughts?*

You kill yourself, the voice answered. *There's really nothing to it.*

You should try it.

Creighton decided to ignore the voice. He picked up one of the few remaining torches and turned, heading east down Main Street.

You can try to keep your thoughts off of this if you want, see where it gets you.

The voice was *audible* in Creighton's mind now, as if the words were being whispered directly into his ear. It caused him to jump when it first crept back with such force. The thing—*Jace*—was taunting Creighton, but the question was: for what reason?

He waved his torch around and turned to peer down each alley, behind every house and shop. He wasn't sure if this area had been searched already, but he also knew the thing could be anywhere.

Fort Whipple is too condensed, he thought. *Too packed together. Something like this was bound to happen.*

The voice cackled inside his mind.

Something like me only comes around once a lifetime, Sheriff.

Creighton hated Buck Phillips in that moment. It wasn't just that he'd gotten so drunk that he was physically unable to help in the search. He'd also gotten so drunk he'd allowed a young boy to trick him. But why had Ambrose let Freeman go?

And why hadn't he called the boy out on it?

Because you're spineless, just like your friend...

Creighton froze. A bloodcurdling scream erupted from close by. He gathered his wits and took off running toward the sound, all the while wondering: *what does that mean, just like my friend? What friend?*

Then came calling and shouting from a nearby group, signaling trouble—as if everyone in a half-mile radius hadn't heard the ruckus.

Predators calling for help as they honed in on the kill.

Or was it the other way around?

"Hey!" He called out as he rounded the corner. "Wait!" He saw a group of three with torches held high, heading down a small alley between two houses.

"Sheriff! Nice of you to join us. We found the bastard!" Travis Gregory called. He was a wiry old man who spent his days running the feed store at the edge of town.

Presently, he stood with a double-barrel shotgun at the ready. "Let's go end this."

Creighton shook his head. "No... no, this is all wrong. Something—" He fell to his knees then as a terrible wailing filled his ears. No, his mind. "Ahh! Make it stop! Make it fucking stop!" Shocks of convulsion shook him as he face-planted in the dirt, writhing in agony.

You can't stop this.

Every muscle in Creighton's body tensed and contracted. He struggled for air as his mind and body seared with white-hot pain.

Travis knelt down, placing his shotgun on the ground. "He's having a fit!"

Creighton could hear them talking about him. He could hear the woman in the group crying, asking what was wrong with him, but he could do nothing to reply. He was seemingly locked in place.

It felt as if his brain was melting in his skull. But the laughing...

Get out of my head!

And just as abruptly as he'd fallen to the ground in agony, he now found that the pain had disappeared. He lay on his back clutching his head in his hands, hat covered in dirt and strewn to the side—it was the lowest moment of his life.

Travis extended a hand. "What in the world was that all about?"

For an old store clerk, Travis was strong. He yanked Creighton off the ground with little trouble. The young couple helped steady Creighton as he swayed like a drunk.

"I..." Creighton began, feeling his heart race in his chest.

Jace. He's playing with me like a cat with an injured mouse.

"...I'm not sure."

Travis bent over and picked up Creighton's hat, brushing it off on his pants leg. "Here you go."

Creighton took the hat with a nod. "Thanks, partner. I'm sorry about that. I don't..." He placed the hat back on his head, straightened it, and shook his head. "Doesn't matter. Let's go."

Travis held up a dirty hand. "Wait. Are you sure you're alright, Sheriff? I mean, you've got a loaded gun and—"

Creighton held up a hand. "I'm fine."

Are you?

The voice was there. Always there. Creighton felt like reaching his hand into the side of his head and yanking it straight out of his brain. He'd start one finger at a time.

A quick rupture of the eardrum would be painful, but oh, *the silence.*

"Sheriff!"

"Oh, my god!"

"Grab him!"

Creighton's hands shook in little tremors as he realized he'd been holding his pistol to his ear. He had no memory of placing it there. He shuddered at the thought that he may not even be in control of his own actions anymore.

I've lost my fucking mind.

He quickly holstered his weapon, ignored the confused and horrified stares of his companions, and rounded the corner where he could bear witness to the bloody, shrunken old man on the ground.

"Is this your masterpiece?" Creighton said aloud. There was nobody there—no one *alive.*

Creighton wasn't oblivious to the terrified reactions of his group. He heard them. He was looking at the same thing as them. The broken window, the trail of blood and entrails.

His expressionless face simply stared at all of it.

Shrill screams hurt Creighton's ears, but he still heard Jace's answer:

You have not even seen a hint of my masterpiece yet.

The night is coming to a close.

Freeman felt stronger than he had in years, but he could feel the surge of energy fading slowly. Even so, the feeling had nearly brought a tear to his eye.

He felt... *alive.*

Maybe that wasn't the right word, alive. After all, that hadn't been the case for centuries. He hadn't had a particularly bad post-life, though. He'd traveled the world, bettering the cause of The Order. He'd seen unbelievably beautiful scenic landscapes—and just as many gorgeous, warm women. He'd loved and lost...

Is this the light that flashes before my eyes?

He huffed a short laugh through his nostrils. What did it even mean... for a vampyre to *die?* There certainly hadn't been any white light when he'd been turned.

Who knows, maybe this is Hell.

Movement caught the corner of Freeman's eye, then, down below, near a large brown barn just outside of town. He swooped as fast as his wings would carry him—he marveled at the feeling of flying; it had been so very long.

It was against the wishes of The Order, after all, that wings be used at any time, for any reason. The amount of feeding needed from small game to maintain flight energy was unsustainable. It meant for a lot of lost life—many times, especially during a *blood frenzy,* it meant the loss of human lives. Add to that the very sight of the wings drives such dreadful fear in the average human. It's typically for the best they stay concealed.

The wind felt good rushing against Freeman's face as he swooped low and landed. He recognized this place as the Jenkins Farm. It had provided sustenance for Freeman during his time in the desert, stalking Jace to this godforsaken place.

The sound of buzzing flies filled the air, and Freeman moved in closer to investigate. The movement had been from behind the barn earlier. There had been something like a gurgled scream as well, but Freeman couldn't be sure.

It felt like old times, Freeman noted—hunting down his prey. He could do it now, he knew that. He could end the boy for what he'd done. It wasn't something he *wanted* to do.

It was demanded of him.

Jace stepped out from behind the barn, holding a bloody kitchen knife in one hand. Doing a little bow, he said, "You're just in time. I even saved you a front-row seat."

What has he done?

"I led you here, that's what I did. You're so predictable, old man." Jace's grip on the bloody knife tightened. "You will never be able to stop me. You can't stop *this.*" He gestured his arms behind him. "Welcome to the beginning of the New Order."

Freeman took a step forward. "I'm not afraid of you." He nodded to the barn. "What's back there, Jace?" Looming shadows danced and were accompanied by thick black smoke.

Jace smirked. "Some may call it my masterpiece. I prefer simply to think of it as a message."

"A message?"

"Soon enough, you'll see. This is only the beginning. Once they all know what I've done. *What I'm capable of!*" He shifted the knife from one hand to the other. "Well, they'll all bow to me, The Order included."

Freeman shook his head. "No. You're not making any sense, Jace. This is just the *frenzy* talking."

Jace laughed. It was a dark, maniacal sound that gave Freeman a chill. "The *frenzy*. Bah!" He spit on the ground. "I hate to break it to you, old man, but you're mistaken."

"But... It didn't make any sense. All the signs of the *frenzy* were there. If that wasn't it..."

The Order had, of course, warned against dissent, particularly among the younger vampyres. The times were constantly changing, and some of the more progressive views of The Order were not appreciated equally by all—especially when it came to walking on eggshells around humans.

As if echoing his thoughts, Jace crooned, "These people are mindless, unenlightened swine, and you know it. They're racist, dumb herd animals." Just then, a sickly looking cow stomped into view, its ribcage visible in the firelight from behind the barn. Freeman could see the thing's red eyes staring at him from twenty yards away.

"They're gazelle. And we are lions. I'm just tired of pretending I'm not. Surely you can understand?"

Freeman had heard all of these arguments before. None of them led to any sort of peaceful outcome. It was the kind of thinking that made the need for The Order's intervention in the first place.

He shook his head, let out a sigh. "You've lost your goddamn mind. I can still remember the days when our kind were burned at the stake publicly for even the slightest suspicion. In those days, we were *murderers*. Killers, and nothing more. That's why we adapted." He knew this was his last chance at a peaceful ending to all of this. He had to try.

He held out a hand toward Jace. "Come on, we can get the hell out of here and never look back. It's not too late to rethink all of this."

Jace appeared to consider this for a moment while more undead livestock slowly made their way out from behind the barn like some macabre parade of death. Freeman's mind drifted to the task at hand. It all depended on the next thing out of Jace's mouth.

Jace sighed. "Somehow, I knew you wouldn't understand. You're just like the rest of them—weak. It's pitiful."

"So, what? You're just going to go around destroying lives and communities as you please? How long do you think that will work for you?"

For the first time, Freeman noticed a hint of weakness flash across Jace's face.

Has he really not thought this through? And he claims not to be in his frenzy.

"I'm not concerned about the humans." He shifted the knife back to his left hand. "I'm not concerned about you or The Order, either. Now, if you don't mind, I need to place some finishing touches on my work." He turned away and Freeman took his chance, diving forward and grabbing for the handle of the knife.

Jace's wings erupted from his back just as Freeman was about to reach the knife, knocking him back onto his ass. Jace wheeled around and drove the knife down at Freeman's throat, missing by only inches as Freeman rolled out of the way. He got to his feet, reached for his own knife, but found the holster was missing.

It must have come off while I was in the air.

He couldn't show his dismay. He had to keep his cool.

Jace lunged again, and Freeman grabbed his arm, twisting it hard behind Jace's back. Freeman grimaced as the bloody knife scraped along his forearm, opening his flesh. Jace thrashed violently and it took all of Freeman's strength to hold him in place—and, more importantly, to keep the knife from doing more damage.

Jace bucked like an angry bull as Freeman drove a knee hard into his back. "You're making a mistake worse than you could possibly imagine!" His face was in the dirt now, each exhalation sent a cloud of dust flying.

"No, I'm taking care of a mistake." Freeman grabbed Jace's knife arm and pushed down as hard as he could, driving the blade deep into his side. The screams were more animal than human.

Does he know?

Freeman nearly jumped as Jace's voice filled his head. He was somehow reading his thoughts, something he'd never been able to do before. Something Jace seemed well trained in.

Freeman drove the knife in further. "Do I know what?"

Jace turned, and Freeman saw his eyes again. Those eyes now looked tired. Pained.

The thud-thud of an approaching horse cart broke Freeman's concentration and Jace took his chance. He lunged forward and opened his jaw wide, revealing deadly fangs. He bit down hard on Freeman's throat, tearing open a gash all the way down to Freeman's shoulder before shoving him to the ground and exploding high into the night sky.

Freeman held his hands to his neck, feeling the cold, black blood ooze through his fingers and hearing it splatter on the ground below. "Is this it? Is this the end of me?"

Defeated.

He looked up to see a familiar face approaching.

Creighton hopped off his trusty horse, feeling like a shell of a man. "Stay, Frank."

The horse made a low chuffing sound, already backing away from the scene. Smoke billowed over the property as the barn had now caught fire. Before him, a wounded Freeman sat on the ground, making small choking sounds. "Don't move, I'm coming over there."

You're getting so close to my masterpiece.

There was that evil hissing in his ear again. It had led him out here, after all.

But what happened to your companions?

Creighton found he couldn't remember.

I'd been standing in that poor man's backyard...and then...

He shook his head. "Fuckin' booze."

Oh, come on, Sheriff. You know what you did.

Creighton ignored the voice, scaled a small wooden fence, and approached Freeman. The ground was sprayed with dark, almost coagulated blood. Too much blood. Creighton's hands shook, and he realized he'd still been holding the pistol. He placed it in its holster. "How are you not dead?"

Freeman uttered a small groan and moved his hand gingerly from the wound. Creighton watched with amazement as the hole slowly began to close. Skin wove itself over muscle, blood dried around the gash, acting as a sealant. "Who says I'm not?"

Creighton nodded slowly. "What *are you*? What is Jace?" His mind whirled. "How did you escape the jailhouse?"

Freeman reached up for a hand, and Creighton helped him to his feet. To Creighton's wonderment, the wound had closed completely now. "No time. I have to go." Freeman's face wore a look of solemn intensity. "I have to end him." He turned to face Creighton one last time. "Be careful."

And then he was gone. He'd leapt straight into the air, unfolded massive, terrifying wings, and disappeared into the dark night sky.

I'm seeing things again. This is all a big hallucination.

Evil-looking animals had all but surrounded Creighton now, a look of insane hunger in their eyes. He brushed his hand down in one swift motion and came back up with his pistol. He fired a couple rounds into the head of a large black goat that was getting dangerously close.

The shots only slowed the animal the slightest bit, and just like Freeman's wound, the bullet holes quickly closed.

Oh my god.

Another goat was approaching from Creighton's left, and more animals still came pouring out from behind the barn.

I'm outnumbered.

The voice laughed in Creighton's mind. *And why is that, Sherriff?*

Creighton screamed. "Leave me the fuck alone!" He took off running around the east side of the barn. He smacked his pistol against the side of his head in a fit of rage.

Please, let this nightmare end. Please...

The barn was completely alight now; smoke rose high into the sky. Creighton shielded his eyes from the flames as he rounded the corner of the barn and froze dead in his tracks.

Creighton understood now. He looked upon Jace's masterpiece—his coup de grâce—with unbridled terror coursing through his veins. He found it hard to catch his breath.

Do you remember now, Sheriff? Do you remember what you've done?

"I...I didn't. I...couldn't."

But you did.

Creighton blinked several times. His mouth was almost too dry to speak. "No," he croaked.

The scene before him was some kind of ritual, Creighton assumed. There was Travis from the feed store, and his daughter and her fiancé. They'd been forced into a pose of supplication, hands held together in prayer, their knees on the ground. Their eyes had been removed and replaced with what looked like silver coins. Metal fence posts had been crudely shoved through their bodies at odd angles to keep them in place. And in the center of each of their foreheads, a bullet hole.

Creighton gasped. He remembered now, vaguely, turning to the group of them and firing on them one-by-one.

His hands shook. His voice wavered as he spoke, "That wasn't me, goddamnit! That was *you!*"

The voice laughed.

The rotting, undead animals loomed around, but none of them seemed interested in the sheriff. Creighton's eyes drifted upward to the centerpiece of Jace's creation—to where all the dead faces stared in mock reverence.

A body hung upside down, tied to a wooden post by the ankles. To say it was a body was being generous. It was more of a bloody, pulpy skeleton. The rib cage had been torn open and the person's skin had been draped over the broken ribs and torso in an imitation of bats' wings. Below, a few animals milled about, feeding on innards and blood.

Do you see now, Sheriff? It's the only future for mankind.

Creighton spun in a slow circle, pistol at the ready. He struggled to maintain a foothold in reality.

Is this really happening?

Did I really kill those people?

In the distance, Creighton could hear Frank neighing, but it was all just part of the background. He couldn't be bothered by it. His senses were at an all-time high.

"Why don't you show yourself, you piece of shit?" Creighton shouted. "Come down here and talk to me like a man!" He stood, listening to the strange moaning cries from the farm animals, listening to the crackling of the fire.

It's old man Jenkins up there, I know it.

Creighton felt rocked by waves of paranoia and fear. Flapping of giant, leathery wings filled his ears, seemingly coming from all directions at once.

Sure you don't want to call off the search?

Creighton dropped to his knees, closed his eyes. He couldn't look at any more dead bodies.

Please, let it all go away.

Creighton heard a loud metallic sound from somewhere behind him. He turned, placed one hand on the ground to steady himself.

I've got you now, you son of a bitch.

A shadowy figure appeared next to a knocked-over bucket. Creighton raised his pistol and unloaded his pistol in that direction, praying he could at least wound the bastard. He heard a loud *thud* as the figure's body hit the ground.

Gingerly, Creighton stood and slowly made his way over to investigate.

Let it all be over.

He checked his pistol—only one more round. "Shit."

Sweat ran down his face and dripped down his back in rivulets—the heat from the fire was nearly overpowering. But that was behind him, and the figure in the brush, completely unmoving—Creighton could tell even in the dim glow that the body was much too small to be Jace's.

Oh, you'd be right about that.

Creighton suddenly stopped. A sudden, chilling revelation came over him then. Jace's masterpiece still wasn't complete. The final pieces were still being placed.

One of them was on the ground in a pool of blood—his own blood.

Ambrose?

He wore a look of shock on his face. Next to his body lay his little.22 pistol he'd been so proud of. No doubt he'd checked on his mama and decided to come help his daddy. That damned stubborn boy.

No, he wouldn't have left her alone. There's no way.

He turned in horror and realized he'd miscounted the bodies staked to the ground in supplication. Old man Jenkins was there, on the far right, stripped naked and murdered on his own land.

It had been his wife and Ambrose's sweet mother, Mary Ann, on display. Creighton had to turn away as the tears flowed for his wife and child.

What have you done, Sheriff? The voice asked. *I told you to back off. I told you I'd make you pay.*

Creighton wailed in desperation. "Why?"

But he knew there was no answer that would make any sense—no justification for the senseless torture, bloodshed, and loss.

"Why?" he asked again in futility. But now the voice in his head was done responding.

Done with him entirely.

Creighton's hands shook uncontrollably as he fumbled with the pistol, barely able to hold it steady as he cocked back the hammer, placed the barrel to his temple, and pulled the trigger.

CHAPTER TWELVE

BUCK PHILLIPS WOKE WITH a start as he heard the metallic keyring crash to the hard wooden floor. "The fuck?"

He rubbed a hand slowly across his face, as if he could wipe the hangover away.

Where the hell am I?

Buck yawned, rubbed his eyes. He was lying on a bed, though it wasn't comfortable in the least—he definitely wasn't home.

Home.

Suddenly he was reminded of Mae, how she'd been so brutally murdered. Then there was that whore, Georgia Dawson, who'd been fucking her behind his back. He remembered that goddamned nigger, too—what was his name?

Freeman.

Buck scoffed. "Free."

He turned his head slowly to survey his surroundings, noting the ache in his neck and back. Springs below him groaned, and he finally realized where he was.

"How in the..." he trailed off. He leaned over the side of the small cot and saw what had woken him—the keys to the cell lay on the floor next to the cot. Using as much energy as he could muster, Buck sat up and looked around the room.

He was alone.

Outside, he could hear shouting, crying. Through the small window by the front door, he could tell it was still mostly dark outside, the sun would likely break over the mountains soon, shining its harsh light all over Fort Whipple. Revealing the damage after the storm.

Buck groaned and reached down to pick up the key ring. On wobbly legs, he walked to the cell door, picked the correct key, and reached around to let himself out. He'd been drunk before, but he'd never been *woken up inside the jail cell* drunk. It was hard to imagine how it had happened. Unless...

Freeman.

Buck could feel his face reddening, his pulse quickening. "I'm going to kill him," he announced to the empty jailhouse. "Sure as shit, I am."

He stepped out of the now-open cell and ambled over to the desk, grabbing his pistol and his hat. He cocked and holstered his pistol and fitted his old hat on top of his head, all the while wondering how he'd been bested.

He belched. A hot stink filled the air. "I swear I'm never drinking again."

That, of course, had not been the first time he'd uttered such a statement. And now with Mae gone...His hands clenched into fists. Before heading out the door, he reached down and opened one of the desk drawers, pulling out a rolled cigarette and a box of matches. He sighed, thinking of Mae as he struck the match and ignited the tobacco.

I can't keep any promises.

Dragging on the cigarette, he shrugged and grabbed the liquor bottle off the desk, took a good-luck swig. "Hair of the dog," he muttered.

It had gone quiet outside, and Buck made his way toward the door to investigate. Slowly, he pushed the door open and held it open for a moment, listening. There was the sound of a horse or two galloping far off, chickens from someone's backyard. Nothing out of the ordinary.

Where the hell did everyone go?

And then an odd thought tugged at him.

Did I imagine all of that shouting? The crying?

He took another drag of the cigarette and shook his head slowly. "What the fuck is goin' on 'round here?" He spit on the ground, tossed the cigarette.

It occurred to Buck when he had to hold on to the support beams of the jailhouse to keep from falling over that he was still wasn't sober. It was no matter. He was an amazing shot with his pistol. He *never* missed. And if truth be told, he'd spent plenty of time target shooting after kicking back a few.

I just need to gather my wits. I'm fine.

Holding on to the railing, he took his first step down the small staircase leading to the street. Then another, and another.

Success.

He stopped at the bottom of the stairs and stood in the street, listening for any sign of where the black stranger could be.

Quiet.

Buck jeered, "Where y'at, you black devil? Don't tell me you're too scared to face me!" He stood and listened, watching for any movement down either end of the street, but there was nothing. He took off toward the east end of town, his hand on his pistol. Each step was a dangerous gamble.

"Gon' kill 'em," Buck said to no one. Then, louder, "I said, 'where are you at, you murderin' nigger?' Come fight me like a ma... ooh!" There had been a sound, like a rug being shaken in the wind. So quick, so precise, and then Buck had found himself on the ground, the breath knocked out of him. When he looked up, he saw Freeman standing over him.

The black man held a finger to his mouth, hissed, "What the hell are you doing? Are you crazy? You're going to get yourself killed."

Buck grinned. His plan had worked. He'd attracted his prey with ease—Freeman was the rat, and Buck was dangling the cheese, luring him in for a swift death.

Or a slow one. Buck didn't care much either way.

"*You.*" The word rolled off Buck's tongue like something poisonous. "You killed my wife; my Mae. And for that, you have to pay."

Freeman's eyes glazed over in shock as Buck emptied three rounds into his chest through the end of the holster at his hip. The echo of the shots rang out across the buildings and danced its way down the street. Buck watched in glee as Freeman collapsed on the ground, moaning in pain.

Buck stood over the good-for-nothing nigger now. "I got you, you piece of shit. Just like I told you I would."

He aimed the pistol again and emptied the rest of the rounds into Freeman's head.

There wasn't a word Freeman was aware of to describe the severity of agonizing pain he was experiencing. Each gunshot was another tiny death. He could feel the wounds closing, some leaving bullets inside his body. His screams were muffled, only slightly, as he rolled over in the dirt, covering himself in black, sticky blood.

A million things raced through Freeman's mind at that moment. His real life, before The Order. Before *the change*. Memories flashed through of the smiling faces of children and partners long gone. He recalled the change. He'd been turned against his will at the age of eighteen by a vagrant vampyre, some homeless blood-sucker wandering the streets.

The man had attacked Freeman while he slept. He'd never forget the sight of his open bedroom window, his partner at the time cowering in the corner while Freeman fought the man off him.

He'd never seen so much blood in all his life—up to that point, of course. Now blood was everything. It was the curse and the blessing.

The memories changed then, scrolling in front of his mind's eye. He was a young vampyre, fresh off his *blood frenzy,* and he had one thing on his mind: women.

He'd met a beautiful young lady in New York shortly after arriving off a long overseas journey with a few of his companions. They'd had to hide for the long, treacherous journey below deck amongst the cargo, feeding on rats the whole way. He remembered The Order being very clear that America was a new country, and she needed guidance from them to calm tensions. America was just getting started as a country, and black men, Freeman found, were not treated fairly in most places.

But the woman, the young lady from New York, with her pale skin, her dark blue eyes and jet black hair—she'd treated him right for a few glorious evenings.

Freeman snapped back to the present, aware suddenly that Buck Phillips was standing over him. He struggled to pull himself to his feet, staggered by the amount of black blood staining the dirt-covered street. Then he heard the familiar sound of wings *whooshing*. Freeman looked up and saw Jace's figure, mere seconds before Buck was snatched by the shoulders and carried straight up into the sky until both of them disappeared.

Freeman spun around, too weak to fly off himself. He glanced over to the mountain range to the east.

Here comes the sun.

It had been a long day and night, and Freeman was so very tired.

Tired of stalking, tired of the constant need for blood, tired of fighting.

But mostly, he was just flat-out exhausted. He was over two-hundred years old, after all.

Buck's screams and curses got quieter, and quieter still, until they were no longer audible. Freeman tried to look up into the sky, but neither of them could be seen.

I tried to tell that old fool to stop attracting attention.

And then the screams came back with full force, getting rapidly louder and louder until. . .

WHAM!

Freeman jumped as Buck's body crashed into a nearby horse cart. There was so much blood. Scattered across the street were bits of torn flesh, entrails, an eyeball leaking fluid onto the ground. Warm, red blood misted Freeman's face, and he dared to wipe his hand across it and lick his fingers. It felt good, but he was still too weak to do much of anything.

So it's come to this, Freeman thought. *Sitting around, waiting to get picked off by my own...*"Oh my god," he uttered.

Jace landed in front of him then. "That's right. You finally figured it out."

Tears welled in Freeman's eyes as he came to the awful realization. It was right in front of him the whole time, but he'd been too blind to see it.

Jace continued, "My mother died giving birth to me alone in a dark room in New York City." He shot a dirty look in Freeman's direction. "I never knew *my father.*"

Please stop talking.

"I spent my whole life hating *you.* I hated you for what you did to her—for what I was born as. I hated you for making me an orphan and a freak at the same time. And then what did you do? You moved on to the next city to fuck the next willing woman, didn't you?" He barked a short laugh. "And did you, for once, stop to think about the consequences? Of the lives you ruined?"

It hit Freeman like a sledgehammer to the chest. The light skin, the eyes...the *anger.* The *blood frenzy* as well...they only occur when a human is changed *after* birth.

It would also explain Jace's strength and power. It was rare these days for a vampyre to be born as one.

And the boy's poor mother... what had been her name?

"I-I..." Freeman stammered. "I was young. I didn't know. I'm so sor—"

Jace interrupted. "Her name was Julia, or so they told me. I never got a chance to meet her. I was never able to talk with her, to see her smiling face. All because of *you.*"

"We can make this work, Son."

"Don't you *dare* call me that," Jace sneered. "And no, we can't. I'm afraid our paths are very different, and now that you know of my power, you can go back to The Order and let them know things will be changing."

Tears hit the ground where Freeman stood. He didn't know what to say, what to do. His mind raced with all the possibilities, all outcomes.

What can I say that hasn't already been said?

"I'm afraid I can't do that, Jace. You know that."

Jace uncrossed his arms, nodded. "Well then, I guess it's time we find out who gets to walk away from this."

Freeman knew what Jace meant. He knew Jace understood Freeman's orders, and at the same time, that the boy would never surrender. He'd gone too far, the body count too high. Even if Freeman somehow could save him from this mistake, The Order would surely have him burned at the stake for these crimes against humanity. Of course, Freeman had killed plenty during his *frenzy,* but this was different.

This would have no natural end.

Jace lunged toward Freeman, grabbing him, and wrestling with him. Freeman fell to the ground, hard, crying out in pain as he was slammed down against his gunshot wounds.

A crowd had gathered now, watching the spectacle.

"Over here!"

"They're fighting!"

Freeman fought back, turning over on top of Jace and pinning him to the ground. He could *feel* his energy depleting—it took everything in him to hold him down. He looked down and saw the shock on Jace's face. He saw tears in his eyes.

Already, Freeman's plan was about to come to fruition. He remembered his instructions from Mother Kynes. He knew the damage was too great to save the boy.

He didn't know he wouldn't be able to save himself.

Right now, he didn't want to.

The first ray of sunlight shone over Main Street in Fort Whipple, and Freeman looked back to his long-lost son. "I wish things could have been different."

Jace turned his head to face the sunlight head-on, tears streaming his burning face as he held on tightly to his father. "I know," he said.

Afterword

As soon as I saw the first release in Death's Head Press's splatter western series, I knew I wanted to write one of my own, to be a part of the impressive list of my peers who would contribute their own version of a good old, demented western story.

If I'm honest, it wasn't easy writing this one. As many of you know, my mom passed in April of 2020, and it really took a lot out of me. If you managed to make it to the end of this book, it may be evident from the very words on the page—I was going through a lot.

I'm happy to say my mental health is leagues better now as I write this, in December of 2021. It feels amazing to have another book ready to go out into the world—one of my *own*, of course. On top of that, I'm proud of this one.

I want to thank everyone who has stuck by me during the dark times, when I didn't have much to say. Thank you for checking out my work again.

I promise there's a lot more to come soon.

Who knows, maybe we'll see Freeman again, in a past life.

—Justin
Dec 17, 2021